THE HUTCHINSON BOOK OF

Mouse Tales

HUTCHINSON

London Sydney Auckland Johannesburg

THE HUTCHINSON BOOK OF MOUSE TALES
A HUTCHINSON BOOK 0 091 89358 5

Published in Great Britain by Hutchinson,
an imprint of Random House Children's Books

This edition published 2004

1 3 5 7 9 10 8 6 4 2

RANDOM HOUSE CHILDREN'S BOOKS
61–63 Uxbridge Road, London W5 5SA
A division of The Random House Group Ltd

RANDOM HOUSE AUSTRALIA (PTY) LTD
20 Alfred Street, Milsons Point, Sydney,
New South Wales 2061, Australia

RANDOM HOUSE NEW ZEALAND LTD
18 Poland Road, Glenfield, Auckland 10, New Zealand

RANDOM HOUSE (PTY) LTD
Endulini, 5A Jubilee Road, Parktown 2193, South Africa

THE RANDOM HOUSE GROUP Limited Reg. No. 954009
www.kidsatrandomhouse.co.uk

A CIP catalogue record for this book is available from the British Library.
Book design by Ian Lansley and Clair Stutton

Printed in China

Contents

Town House Mouse
How we lived 100 years ago

Nigel Brooks and Abigail Horner

DOOR KEY

MY NAME is Augustus John
Town Mouse. I'd like to show
you round our house.

WELCOME

I live here with my family: Mama, Papa and sister Kate, and baby brother Gregory; and Potts, the butler, Mrs Jones, the cook, our nanny, kind Miss Adelaide, and Rose, the under-parlour maid.

The year is 1900. Come inside . . .

PAPA, MAMA AND BABY GREGORY

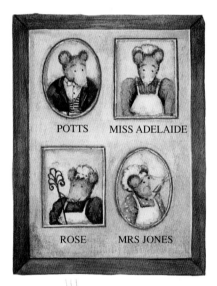

POTTS   MISS ADELAIDE

ROSE   MRS JONES

KATE

ME

GOOD MORNING

MY BED

KATE'S BED

In the early morning, when we are still cosy in our beds, the servants are already up and hard at work.

Rose brings us up a tray of tea and toast, then runs downstairs to empty our chamber pots in the bathroom at the end of the hall (she doesn't like this job at all!).

SERVICE BELLS

N.E. BEDROOM

N.E. DRESSING ROOM

MASTER BEDROOM

THE STUDY

PAPA'S BREAKFAST TRAY

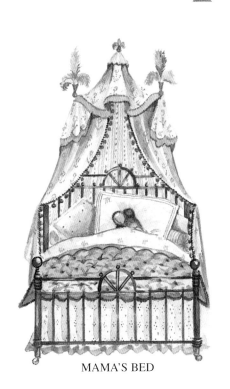

MAMA'S BED

PAPA'S BED

Potts opens the curtains to let in the sun, while down in the kitchen Mrs Jones plans her recipes for the day. Rose cleans out the grates and then lights the fires, sighing, "A parlour maid's work is never done!"

CHAMBER POT

DOORS

Potts, the butler, is in charge of our big front door. When the bell rings he comes hurrying from the hall. Visitors for Mama and Papa leave calling cards. The postman brings our letters and parcels. I'm waiting for a parcel from my Uncle Teddy in America.

LETTERS

UNCLE TEDDY'S PARCEL

WATCHING TRAMS

WILBERFORCE WHISKERS' CALLING CARD

DOOR KEY

CLEANING THE STEPS

RAILINGS

OUR FRONT DOOR

OUR BACK DOOR

THE DRESSMAKER

THE GROCER

THE CHIMNEY SWEEP

Our back door is called the tradesmen's entrance. The doorbell never stops ringing. It's here the servants go in and out. And all day long the tradespeople bring the things we need to keep our big house running smoothly.

THE COALMAN

THE BAKER'S BOY

THE MILKMAN

OUR CLOTHES

Woolly drawers that button down
Collars and cuffs that come off to wash
Boots and shoes and caps and hats
Smart tweed suit for round the town
Handkerchiefs and silk cravat
My favourite sailor suit and hat.

Muslin bloomers and camisole
Stockings, gloves and cotton smock
Drawstring purse and party frock
For summer a pink parasol
A warm wool coat for winter-time
A sailor suit that matches mine.

THE SCHOOL ROOM

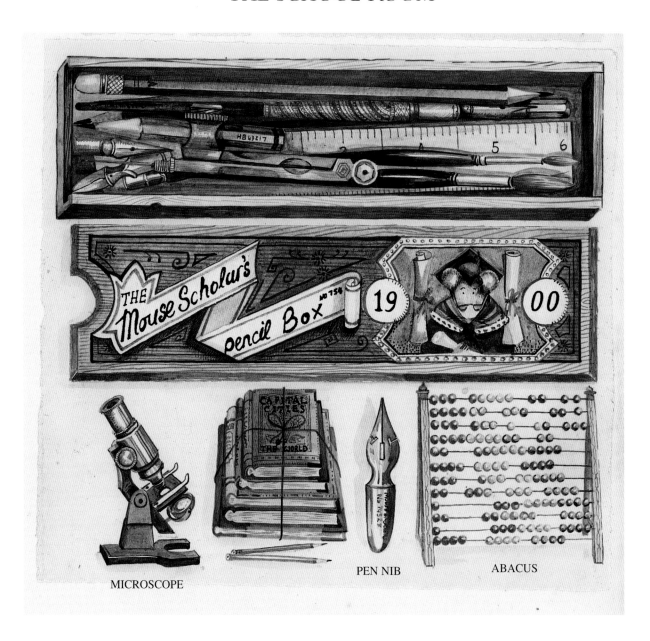

MICROSCOPE

CAPITAL CITIES OF THE WORLD

PEN NIB

ABACUS

We don't go out to school. Our governess, Miss Algebra, comes every morning at eight o'clock. We must be good, we mustn't fight, and if we can't get our sums all right and recite our capital cities one by one, she might rap our knuckles with a ruler.

A a B b C c

MAMA'S DRESSING ROOM

CURLING TONGS

JUG AND BASIN

MAMA'S BLOOMERS

TORTOISESHELL COMB

Getting ready's such a fuss
Mirror, brush and powder puff
Bottles filled with sweet perfume
Diamond rings and ivory comb
Petticoats and underskirts
Corset pulled so tight it hurts.

CORSET TO MAKE
MAMA THIN

HAIR BRUSH

VIOLET
face
WATER

Wrinkle
Cream

There's a dress Mama has seen in a chic French magazine. Our seamstress took the picture home and made one that looked just the same. Yards and yards of rose-pink satin – Mama's now ready for her fitting.

THIMBLE

SEWING BOX

PIN CUSHION

THE LATEST HAND-OPERATED
SEWING MACHINE

TAPE MEASURE

PAPA'S STUDY

The study is Papa's private place and he hates to be disturbed. He reads the newspapers, writes his letters, and checks his accounts. Sometimes, though, we are allowed inside and he tells us stories of his adventures as a captain in the navy.

When I grow up I'll be a sailor too and sail the seven seas.

INK BLOTTER

PAPA'S PIPE

LETTERS

SPECTACLES

INK BOTTLE

Town House Mouse — Nigel Brooks and Abigail Horner

PAPA'S SHIP THE
BLACK MOUSE

CAST-IRON CLOCK

BIG BRASS TELESCOPE

WRITING BUREAU

THE GARDEN SQUARE

The park is across our busy road where trams rattle up and down all day.

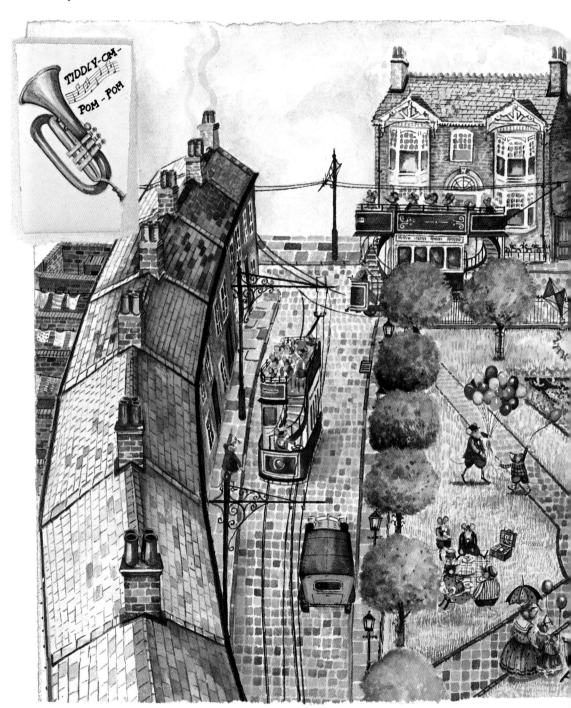

There are flowers and trees and a big bandstand. In summer we go for an afternoon stroll. Nanny pushes Gregory in his pram and when no one's looking holds hands with her young man.

LEAD URN

PARASOL

MY POND YACHT

THE NURSERY

Although we're no longer babies, our playroom is still called the nursery. A rocking horse, a spinning top, china dolls, a ball and cup, a cheeky money-box tin mouse, and Kate's doll house with miniature furniture.

KATE'S MINIATURE
MOUSE TOY
DOLL HOUSE

My toy train that rattles round and round
the track, a clockwork ship with a big brass
key. Our tin soldiers fight famous battles –
blue for Kate and red for me.

MOUSETANIC

TOOT TOOT

MARBLES

COOK IN HER KITCHEN

Our cook, Mrs Jones, is the queen of the kitchen, with batteries of pots and pans at her command.

With Rose to help, she cooks for everyone. Sometimes (she says) she wishes she had twenty pairs of hands. We love to help her make the dough for her puddings and pies, but most of all the cakes so we can lick the sticky spoon.

All the servants eat downstairs – their breakfast, lunch, tea and supper. Here Potts pours the wine into a crystal jug to serve upstairs, and polishes the silver.

GRATER

BIG, STICKY WOODEN SPOON

BRASS PATENT Nº 758 STEAMER

CRYSTAL JUG

POTTS POLISHES THE SILVER

MRS JONES PUTS ROSES MADE FROM
ICING ON TOP OF HER CAKE

ROLLING PIN

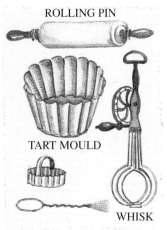

TART MOULD

WHISK

MECHANICAL
FRUIT PEELER

ROSE SHINES THE TABLE
KNIVES WITH A MACHINE
CALLED THE SERVANT'S FRIEND

DINNER TIME

We eat with Nanny upstairs in the nursery: steak-and-kidney pie or cheese-and-onion flan.

On Fridays fish is always served (it's good for us says Nan). Tonight Mama and Papa have important visitors.

And downstairs they are served from silver dishes and eat from porcelain plates: roast beef and creamed potatoes and afterwards trifle and great big cakes. When we're grown up Mama says we can sit at table too, but that seems a long, long time to wait!

ENTERTAINMENT

Sometimes Mama and Papa hold a ball. We're not allowed downstairs, but we creep out into the hall and hope we won't be seen. Secretly, we listen to the grown-ups talk, and watch the dancing.

At the end of the day if we are all at home and no one's visiting we sometimes have a game of cards or snakes and ladders, or billiards (which Papa is teaching me to play).

BILLIARDS WITH PAPA

MAMA AND PAPA PLAY WHIST

PUZZLES AND QUIZZES IN
FRONT OF A ROARING FIRE

BATH TIME

MAMA WASHES
HER FACE

PAPA SHAVES HIS WHISKERS

VIOLET

GENTLE
TOILET
SOAP

PAPA'S RAZOR

Our bathroom has a cast-iron tub. Nanny gives our backs a
scrub and washes behind our ears. Papa shaves with foam and
brush. Mama is always in a rush. We have a smart new toilet –
quite the latest thing – with a porcelain cistern and a chain to
pull to make it flush. In the morning there's often a queue, so
we really need another one – or two.

BED TIME

Before I lay me down to sleep
I pray the Lord my soul to keep

When we've undressed and said our prayers, Nanny tucks us up in bed and reads to us by gas-light: stories of ghosts and long lost treasure chests or tales from the mummy's tomb . . . we like the scary stories best.

Mama and Papa won't go to bed for hours, but I know that after midnight when we are fast asleep, into our room our mama comes and whispers . . .

NIGHTDRESS

HOT MILKY DRINKS

POT HOT
WATER BOTTLE

SPOOKY HORROR

PYJAMAS

"Good night, my little ones."

Herbert Binns
and the Flying Tricycle

Caroline Castle and Peter Weevers

HERBERT BINNS was very small, even for a mouse, but he didn't care. He could do double somersaults, read backwards, and sing and play the accordion; but what he liked best was inventing. Herbert Binns was a marvellous inventor.

Most animals loved Herbert Binns, but there were three – McTabbity, an old rabbit; Zip, a greedy young rat; and Measly, a mean old weasel – who didn't like him at all. They were jealous that such a small animal could have so many talents. Whenever they saw Herbert, they would taunt him with a cruel rhyme:

"Herbert Binns is so horribly small
That no one cares for him at all."

But Herbert was able to make up rhymes on
the spur of the moment, and he would reply
with something like:

"Herbert Binns may be smaller than you,
But look what this tiny mouse can do!
He goes head over heels, he can play and sing,
And best of all he'll invent anything!"

The three animals could never think
of anything to reply in return and they
would wander off, stamping their feet and
feeling furious that someone so small and unimportant-looking
could be so clever.

One afternoon, Zip, Measly and McTabbity were sitting in their secret den, talking about their favourite subject.

"That Herbert Binns," said McTabbity, "is too small for his boots."

"Have you heard about his latest plan?" said Zip.

"No! What?" said the others eagerly, for the affairs of Herbert Binns were of great interest to them.

"Well," said Zip, lowering his voice to a whisper, "he says he's invented a flying tricycle, and he's going to demonstrate it next Thursday afternoon."

"A flying tricycle!" roared McTabbity in a furious rabbity voice. "Who does he think he is to invent a flying tricycle, indeed?"

Of course, the gang had never thought of inventing a flying tricycle themselves – in fact, they never thought about anything much, except Herbert Binns. Without Herbert to get angry about, their lives would have been quite dull.

So they gathered round to think how Herbert could be taken down a peg or two.

The next day, Herbert Binns was in his workshop, poring over his plans for the flying tricycle. As he worked he sang this song:

"If birds and bees and tops of trees
Are things you specially like,
If you like a breeze around your knees
You'll need Binns' flying trike.

"Mustn't forget my special starting pin," he muttered to himself. "Most important for a smooth takeoff."

What he didn't see, however, was a whiskery face at the window. It was McTabbity, and he was writing down every word that Herbert Binns said.

Zip and Measly were sitting at Vole's waterside café when McTabbity came rushing up. "I have here all we need to fix that mouse," he cried, and he read aloud from his piece of paper.

"Ha!" said Zip, snuffling down a whole glass of barley wine in one go. "Special pin, eh? Let's steal it – then won't he look silly when his wonderful tricycle doesn't take off?"

And he laughed a ratty laugh.

The three animals turned to look at the poster that was stuck on an old willow in the middle of the café:

```
       HERBERT BINNS,
      MOUSE AND INVENTOR,
    WILL BE DEMONSTRATING HIS
   SPECTACULAR FLYING TRICYCLE
     NEXT THURSDAY AFTERNOON
     DOWN BY THE RIVERSIDE.
          ALL WELCOME
```

"That's what he thinks!" sneered McTabbity.

That night, as Herbert Binns slept peacefully in his bed, the three animals crept up to his house. Zip and Measly kept watch, while McTabbity silently squeezed himself through the window of the workshop.

He looked in Herbert's drawers; he looked under the carpet; he looked inside Herbert's box of treasures on the shelf and found – nothing. He was just about to give up when he spotted Herbert's jacket hanging up behind the door. He reached inside the pocket and his claw touched something cold and hard! The special pin!

That very second, an owl hooted and a cloud crept over the moon. McTabbity began to get the jitters. Quickly he grabbed the special pin and scrambled back through the tiny window.

Back in the den with Zip and Measly, McTabbity jumped about in excitement. "Thinks he's clever, that Binns," he chortled. "But some animals are cleverer – namely myself!" And he took the special pin from his pocket.

Zip and Measly looked at McTabbity in admiration. At last Herbert Binns was going to get his comeuppance.

The three animals were so excited that they could hardly wait for Thursday to arrive. Whenever they saw some animals reading the poster, they called out with glee:

"Be sure to be there, be sure to be there,
When the minuscule mouse takes to the air."

Thursday afternoon arrived at last. Down by the riverside, the crowd had gathered, and a banner was tied between two trees which said:

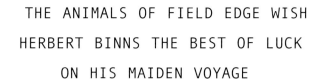
THE ANIMALS OF FIELD EDGE WISH
HERBERT BINNS THE BEST OF LUCK
ON HIS MAIDEN VOYAGE

"He'll need it," sneered McTabbity.

"We couldn't have picked a better plan," said Zip. "The whole of Field Edge is here to watch him make a fool of himself. He won't dare show his whiskery face in public again."

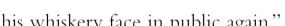

Just at that moment, Herbert Binns came over the hill aboard the most wonderful machine. It was a green tricycle with two enormous wings that flapped beautifully as he pedalled.

Zip, Measly and McTabbity could hardly stop laughing as Herbert reached into his waistcoat pocket.

Then to the animals' amazement, he took out the special pin.

"What . . ?" said Zip.

"How . . ?" said Measly.

"It can't be!" said McTabbity.

Herbert looked at the three animals in turn, then in a sensible mousy voice he said:

"You rabbity McTabbity,
You're dafter than a hare.
You didn't think I'd risk your tricks!
You see – I've got a spare!"

And with that he inserted the special pin and the flying tricycle glided into the air as gracefully as a bird.

McTabbity, Zip and Measly raged and gnashed their teeth.

"We'll get him next time," said Measly.

"Never fear," said Zip.

"That stupid . . ." screamed McTabbity.

But we'll never know what he said because
his voice was drowned by the cheers of
the crowd as Herbert Binns, the wings
of his tricycle flapping beautifully,
disappeared over the tops
of the trees.

Look Out, Patrick!

Paul Geraghty

ONE BREEZY afternoon
Patrick was strolling home.

It was a lovely day, the birds
were singing and there was a
spring in his step.

"The world is such a
pleasant place," he said.

**OH NO, PATRICK!
LOOK OUT!**

He gazed about in wonder.

The countryside was full of delightful surprises.

The smell of new grass, the fresh green leaves and ripe red berries just ready to eat.

OH NO, PATRICK! LOOK OUT!

He bent down to sniff
at a buttercup.

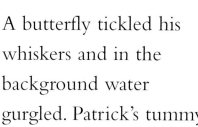

Bumble bees were buzzing
back and forth busily.
The air was sweet with
the scent of nectar.

**OH NO, PATRICK!
LOOK OUT!**

A butterfly tickled his
whiskers and in the
background water
gurgled. Patrick's tummy
began gurgling too.

I wonder what's
cooking in the
cottage, he thought.

**OH NO, PATRICK!
LOOK OUT!**

He tiptoed carefully. That wicked cat might be on the prowl.

There was no sign of the cat. But there was a nice big chunk of cheese.

"Mmmmm," said Patrick.
"Just the thing."

**OH NO, PATRICK!
LOOK OUT!**

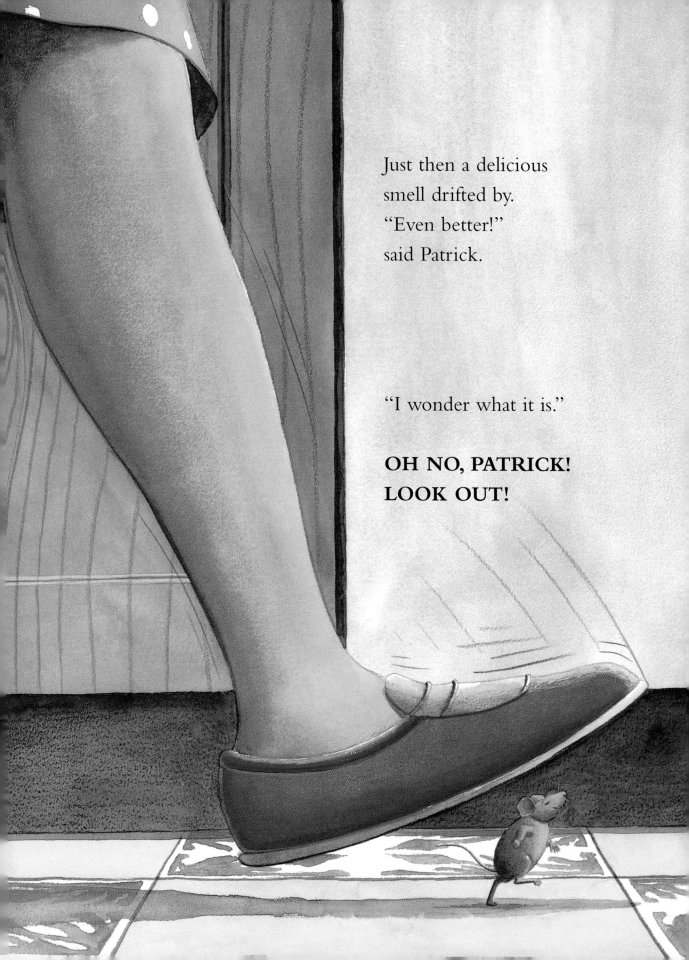

Just then a delicious
smell drifted by.
"Even better!"
said Patrick.

"I wonder what it is."

**OH NO, PATRICK!
LOOK OUT!**

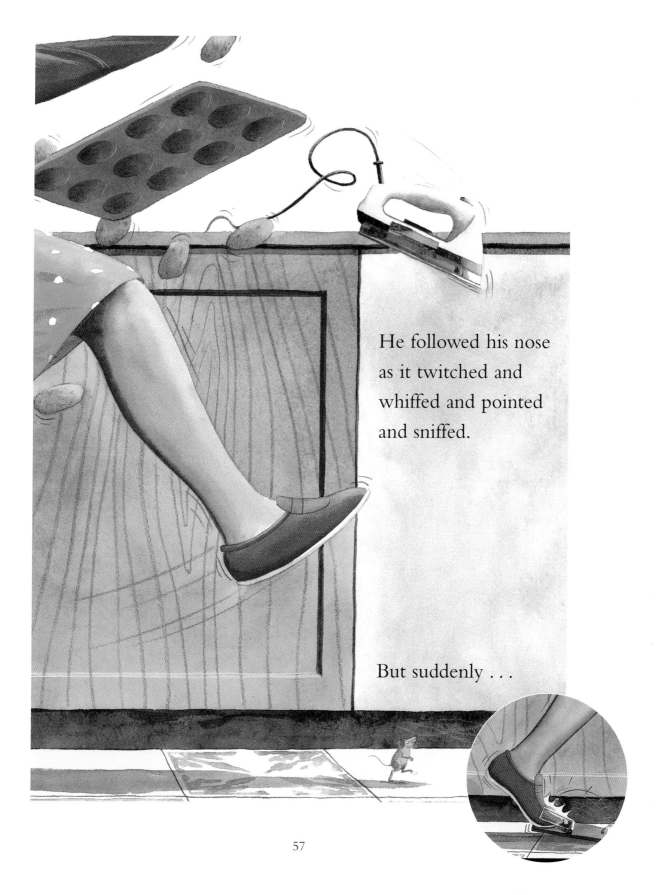

He followed his nose
as it twitched and
whiffed and pointed
and sniffed.

But suddenly . . .

OH NO, PATRICK!
LOOK OUT!

"Phew!
Must be my lucky day!"

Mouse and Mole

Joyce Dunbar and James Mayhew

TALK TO ME

"TALK TO ME," said Mouse.

"What about?" said Mole.

"Anything," said Mouse.

"I can't think of anything," said Mole. "Give me some ideas."

"You could tell me what we are going to do tomorrow," said Mouse.

"What are we going to do tomorrow?" said Mole.

"Well," said Mouse. "If it's a fine day we are going on a picnic in the woods. We are making cheese and cucumber sandwiches.

And we are taking our new picnic basket with cups and saucers and plates."

"So we are," said Mole. "But what if it isn't a fine day?"

"If it isn't a fine day," said Mouse, "we are going to make an apple-wood fire. We will sit in our cosy armchairs and roast chestnuts and toast muffins. We will have hot chocolate to drink."

"So we will," said Mole. "But what if it's an in-between sort of day?"

"We will do something in-between," said Mouse. "We will tidy up."

"So we will," said Mole.

"Thank you for talking to me," said Mouse.

"That's all right," said Mole.

SALAD

Mole's snout peeped out of the bedclothes.

"What sort of day is it?" he asked.

"Wild and wintry," said Mouse.

Mole snuggled his snout back down. "In that case I'll stay in bed."

"Don't you worry," said Mouse. "I will make an apple-wood fire in the sitting room. Then you will want to get up."

Mouse made an apple-wood fire. Mole's snout sniffed apple-wood smoke. Soon he was shuffling downstairs.

"How I hate these wild and wintry days," he grumbled. "All we can do is huddle by the fire."

"We can do more than that," said Mouse.

"We can toast some muffins. We can roast some chestnuts."

"Good," said Mole. "I'm hungry."

So Mouse toasted some muffins and roasted some chestnuts.

"Are there any more?" asked Mole when he had eaten a plateful.

"Are there any more?" Mole asked again when he had eaten a second plateful.

"I've eaten too much," said Mole when he had eaten a third plateful. "Tomorrow I will eat only salad."

"That's a good idea," said Mouse.

"It is," said Mole. "So why wait? I will start my diet now. Have we got any salad, Mouse?"

"We have," said Mouse. "We have carrots, radishes and spinach."

"Then I'll have some," said Mole, and he ate a plateful of salad.

"Aren't I good?" he said. "I have eaten all that salad. I think I deserve a little treat. Butter some muffins, Mouse. Roast a few more chestnuts."

Then Mole ate another plateful. "Wintry days are not so bad after all," he said, falling into a snooze.

TIDYING UP

"Hurray!" said Mouse the next morning. "The sun is shining today. Today we can go on our picnic!"

"No we can't," said Mole. "I ate too much yesterday. I ate toasted muffins and salad. Then I ate more toasted muffins. Today I will eat nothing at all. I will do exercises instead."

But when Mole went into the sitting room to do his exercises, he found it was all of a clutter.

"We will have to tidy up, Mouse. I need some space to bend and stretch."

So Mouse bent down and picked all the clutter up from the floor. Mole collected all the bits and bobs from the shelves. Mouse cleared away all the odds and ends from the sofa. They piled everything into the kitchen.

"There!" said Mouse when they had finished. "Now there's room for you to bend and stretch!"

"But what about my deep breathing?" said Mole. "I need fresh air for deep breathing. Here there is too much dust. We will have to dust and sweep, Mouse."

So Mouse got down on his four paws and swept the floor. Mole stretched on tiptoe to dust the cobwebs off the ceiling and shelves. They worked so hard that soon they were out of breath.

"Phew!" panted Mouse when they had finished. "I'm puffed. But now you can do your exercises."

"Exercises!" said Mole. "I'm too exhausted to exercise! What I need is a cup of tea. Come on, Mouse. Follow me into the kitchen. We deserve a cup of tea."

But when they went into the kitchen to make a cup of tea, they found it all of a clutter.

"Mouse," said Mole. "We will have to tidy up. There's no room to make a cup of tea."

So together they tidied up the kitchen. They scooped up all the bits and bobs.

They gathered in all the odds and ends. Then they bundled them into the bedroom. It took them the rest of the day.

"There!" said Mole when they had finished. "We've tidied up the sitting room. We've tidied up the kitchen. We deserve a cup of tea and something to eat as well. How about pancakes and treacle?"

So Mouse made a pile of pancakes while Mole got out a tin of treacle.

"I need an early night after that," said Mole when he had finished.

"So do I," said Mouse.

But when they went into the bedroom for their early night, they found it was all of a clutter.

"Mouse," said Mole. "Just look at my bed. It is covered with odds and ends."

"And just look at mine," said Mouse. "It is piled with bits and bobs."

They flopped into bed just the same. They were much too tired to care . . .

STUFF

"Help!" cried Mole the next morning. "I am being buried alive."

"I know just how you feel," said Mouse. "Come on. We will have to tidy up."

"But we tidied up yesterday," said Mole.

"We did. But we did it all wrong," said Mouse. "The problem, you see, is stuff. We've got too much stuff. We didn't tidy it up at all. We moved it from room to room. We need to get rid of it altogether."

"But I like stuff," said Mole. "Stuff is very interesting. It might come in useful one day."

"You can have stuff, or you can have space," said Mouse. "But you can't have both."

"But what is the use of space if you have no stuff to put in it?" asked Mole.

"Space is space," said Mouse, "and stuff is stuff. Come on. Let's take some stuff to the rubbish dump and we can have some space for a change. Help me to fill these sacks."

Together they filled three sacks.

"You are right, Mouse," said Mole when they had finished. "Look at all this lovely space. No more tidying up! No more stuff to tidy!"

"We can take these sacks on the motorbike," said Mouse. "Whose turn is it to drive?"

"Mine," said Mole. "Same as last time."

There were three big skips at the rubbish dump. One was marked "Glass". Another was marked "Paper". A third was marked "Metal".

Mouse threw all the newspapers into the skip marked "Paper". "That's that!" he said.

"But look at that bundle of comics," said Mole.
"They look very interesting. I must take them home." And he filled up the sack with old comics.

Then Mouse threw all the empty jars and bottles into the skip marked "Glass". "That's that!" he said.

"But look at that old mirror," said Mole, "and that fish tank. I must take them home. You never know, they might come in useful."

And he put them into a sack.

Mouse threw all the old tin cans and old pans into the skip marked "Metal". "That's that!" he said.

"But look at those coat hangers, and that old tin trunk, and those metal springs. I must take them home. They might come in useful," said Mole.

And he filled up the last of the sacks.

So Mole and Mouse rode home, carrying three sacks full of stuff.

"How clever you are to think of making all that space," said Mole. "Now we have somewhere to put all this stuff."

He tipped the comics onto the floor in the sitting room. He put the fish tank and the mirror on the shelves. He emptied the coat hangers and the tin trunk and the metal springs onto the floor. There was no room left for Mouse and Mole.

Mouse scratched his head.

"As I was saying, Mole, you can have stuff, or you can have space, but you can't have both. We will have to stay outside."

Mouse sat down on the steps. Mole twiddled a broken spring. "I brought this one especially for you," said Mole. But Mouse wasn't pleased. Not a bit!

THE PICNIC

"I think we should go on our picnic today," said Mouse. "I feel like a good long walk."

"So do I," said Mole. "But what about the weather?"

"It's fine," said Mouse. "The sun is shining and there's hardly a cloud in the sky."

"In that case I shall wear my T-shirt and shorts and sun hat," said Mole.

"And I will pack the hamper," said Mouse.

Soon they were ready to go. They had just reached the gate when Mole suddenly stopped stock still.

"I can see a cloud!" he said.

"It's only a little cloud," said Mouse.

"It will soon be a rain cloud. I must put on my mackintosh and galoshes and sou'wester."

While Mouse was waiting for Mole, he couldn't resist a little dip into the hamper. He ate three of the cheese and cucumber sandwiches.

"Here I am!" said Mole at last. "Ready to face any weather! I have my woolly things on top, and my rain things underneath, and my sun things underneath that."

They had walked a little way further when Mole stopped still once more.

"What about my pyjamas?" he said.

"What about your pyjamas?" asked Mouse.

"We might walk so far on our picnic that we might not get back in time for bed," said Mole. "I must go back for my pyjamas just in case."

While Mouse waited for Mole, he couldn't resist a little dip into the hamper. He ate some crisps, some iced buns and two apples.

"Here I am!" said Mole at last. "I have got my pyjamas. And guess what? I have remembered my swimming things as well. You never know, we might find a place to swim."

"But you don't like swimming," said Mouse.

"So I don't," said Mole. "I forgot."

Mouse brushed some crumbs from his whiskers. "Mole," he said. "Have you had a good long walk?"

"Why, yes I have, come to think of it," said Mole. "With all that to-ing and fro-ing."

"Good," said Mouse, "because we are not going on a picnic after all."

"Why not?" said Mole.

"Because I have eaten all the food in the hamper," said Mouse.

"I thought there might be an emergency," said Mole, "so guess what?"

"What?" said Mouse.

"I have packed another picnic in my pockets. Why don't we sit down right here and eat it?"

"You can eat it, Mole. I'm full up. I'm going for a good long walk."

And Mouse did.

The Tale of Admiral Mouse

Bernard Stone and Tony Ross

ONE SUMMER'S evening, as young Tom Tiddler strolled along the shore with his grandfather, he saw a beautiful little ship lying on its side in the sand.

"Can I take it home?" he asked his grandfather.

"Best not," his grandfather replied with a smile, for he knew the ways of the sea. "It may belong to someone. Hold it to your ear and listen to the wind blowing through the rigging. In the wind you will hear the ship's story."

So Tom held the ship to his ear and a famous tale it told.

One terrible day long ago, the English and the French mice decided to raid each other's cheese stores. The French mice declared that all the English cheeses from Cheddar to Stilton belonged to them. And the English mice declared that all the French cheeses from Brie to Camembert belonged to them. Press gangs were sent out to recruit mice to fight for their cheeses.

In England the sailors sadly bade goodbye to their wives and sweethearts and went to their ships that lay at anchor in the bay.

But one mouse refused to be left behind. It was dainty Molly Mouse, wife of the brave Lieutenant Hercules. Disguised as a seaman, she would accompany her husband and stand by his side in the coming battle. Aboard the ships all was confusion. No mouse could be found to lead the fleet. No mouse could think of a plan to defeat the enemy. The great ships lay uselessly in the bay.

Suddenly a ship appeared on the horizon. Slowly, it made its way alongside the other ships. Who could it be? A great cheer went up. It was Admiral Horatio Mouse, the hero of a great many sea battles. He had come to take command. He would lead them against the enemy.

That night a great party took place on all the ships to celebrate the admiral's arrival. The sailors danced hornpipes far into the night.

The next day, Admiral Mouse summoned the four most important captains to attend him. One small mouse rowed them across the choppy water to his flagship.

Admiral Mouse outlined a brilliant plan. He would divide his fleet in two, and trap the enemy between the two halves. He leapt from his chair in his excitement and cried:

"We'll drub the Frenchies from the seas.
We'll teach them not to steal our cheese.
Paris and Calais, Nice and Narbonne,
They'll be sorry when their cheeses are gone."

The fleet set sail that very day, with Admiral Mouse at the helm.

After four days at sea, Lieutenant Hercules Mouse, aboard the leading frigate, finally spied the enemy. Molly stood by his elbows as he signalled to Horatio:

E-N-E-M-Y L-E-A-V-I-N-G P-O-R-T.
W-I-N-D B-L-O-W-I-N-G S-O-U-T-H-E-R-L-Y.
I C-A-N S-M-E-L-L T-H-E-I-R C-H-E-E-S-E-S.

Admiral Mouse sniffed the air. He too could smell the cheeses. Camembert, Brie and Roquefort from France. Burgos, Manchego and Cabrales from Spain. He hoisted his first signal:
P-R-E-P-A-R-E F-O-R B-A-T-T-L-E.

The English fleet approached the enemy lines. It was at 12 noon that day, October 21st, that Horatio Mouse addressed his men:

"England expects that every mouse will do his duty, so –
Prepare to bring me back the Brie,
The Camembert and ripe Ervy.
Seize the cheeses with the holes!
Frenchies' stores make them your goals!"

But Admiral Pierre Mouse, the French Commander, who smelt the approach of the English cheeses, had other ideas. He ordered his men:

"They shall not be allowed to pass, so –
Attack the Double Gloucester,
Blue Stilton and Red Leicester!
Make Horatio's mice look silly.
Sink his precious Welsh Caerphilly!"

And behind the French were their allies the Spanish. They had all got out of bed rather late and Admiral Santa Ana Mouse addressed his men between loud yawns:

"Raid the English cheeses (yawn).
Destroy them as you pleases (yawn).
Let no single crumb remain (yawn),
For the glory that is Spain (yawn)."

Guns were run out on all the ships. The biggest guns on the lower decks, the lighter guns on the middle deck, and the lightest guns on the top deck. Admiral Horatio ordered the first cannon to be fired.

The battle that followed was as fierce as any mouse could remember. First the English seemed to be winning, then the French and Spanish. On all sides, sailors were performing deeds of great courage and gallantry.

The situation was desperate. Admiral Horatio called every mouse on deck. Even the chef padlocked his larder and came up, armed to the teeth.

At one terrible moment, it even seemed that Admiral Horatio Mouse might be lost. A cannon ball burst through the side of his ship. It was only the quick thinking of a captain that saved him.

"Jump!" the captain cried, and by a whisker, they both leapt over the flying ball.

One small mouse who had joined the fighting got extremely wet. In the confusion, a bucket of water used to cool the cannon shot was emptied over his head.

Then, when the fighting was at its fiercest, a fearful shudder shook the ship. It was the beginning of a terrible storm. All the ships tossed and rolled. There was no time for fighting. The great ships were being wrecked and sailors were thrown into the sea.

In the water, the mice clung desperately to pieces of timber. The dreadful battle was forgotten, as friend and foe helped one another. Spanish and French mice helped English mice. English mice helped French and Spanish mice.

Brave Lieutenant Hercules found a barrel from a Spanish ship. He and Molly rode astride it, undaunted by the raging sea.

It seemed there was no hope for the desperate sailors, when suddenly they saw a sail on the horizon. It was Merchant Seaman Mouse steering towards them in his sturdy vessel. With great bravery, he and his crew lowered their boats and rescued every single mouse from the sea.

Aboard Merchant Seaman Mouse's ship, the three admirals were quickly shown to the best room. They were given warm towels and served with the tastiest morsels of cheese. As they sat with their feet in hot mustard baths, they all began to think how much more comfortable they were at peace than at war. Admiral Horatio rose to speak for them all:

> *"Let's stop fighting on the High Seas.*
> *To each of us his country's own cheese.*
> *Battles are boring and tiresome and dull.*
> *We'll go home where our cellars are full."*

He raised his glass to them.

"Atishoo!" he sneezed. "Your good health, gentlemen."

"Atishoo! Salut!" answered Admiral Pierre.

"Atishoo! Felicidad!" echoed the Spanish admiral.

They all drank to it.

And, at the water's edge, Tom Tiddler put his ear closer to the little ship, and he could just make out the sound of clinking glasses as the wind fell silent.

Albert and Albertine
at the Seaside

Colin and Moira Maclean

IT WAS holiday time and Mrs Stilton, Clarice and the twins were on their way to St Ivel on Sea. Father and brother Ernest were to join them later.

"Albertine! Sit down at once!" ordered Mother. "You too, Albert."

"And shut that window!" added big sister Clarice.

The twins sighed and did as they were told. They had been waving their shrimping nets out of the train window to see if they could catch butterflies.

As they got off the train, Albert and Albertine were buzzing with excitement. They had only just recovered from the mumps and couldn't wait to be out and about again.

But poor Clarice felt miserable. She had had mumps too, and her face had swollen up like a dumpling. She had missed lots of parties, outings and picnics and now she was being dragged away to the seaside, leaving all her friends behind. The twins resolved to be extra nice to her.

When they arrived at the house, Cook and Lily the maid were waiting to greet them. The twins rushed upstairs to their room and went straight to the window. Down below was the long sandy beach with its row of bathing huts, glittering blue sea and the jetty with its rowing boats.

"I can't see it, can you?" asked Albert.

"Not a sign," replied Albertine.

They clattered downstairs complaining loudly. The monster sandcastle they had built last summer had disappeared!

"Oh do stop yelling," cried Clarice. "And go and wash those filthy paws."

Albertine pulled a face. "How cross she is!"

"Yes," agreed Albert gloomily. "A fine holiday it's going to be if she goes on like that. We'd better think of something to cheer her up."

After lunch the twins couldn't wait to get to the beach. Mother said Clarice was to take them.

"Oh, no!" wailed Clarice. "Why can't Lily take them? I want to read quietly in my room."

"Not today," said Mother, firmly. "You're still looking pale. The beach will do you good."

The twins led the way, laden with buckets, spades and nets. It was a pity their old fishing rods were broken, but they had already asked Mother for new ones. Whooping for joy they raced to the water's edge, while Clarice settled down to read. "Let's try and find a really whopping flounder for Clarice," suggested Albert. "She'd be sure to like that."

They spent ages catching baby flounders and putting them in their buckets but none seemed quite good enough for their sister. Then, at last, Albertine felt a huge one wriggling in the sand under her toes.

"Here's a beauty! Can you get it, Albert?"

Albert could, and did. He held it up, flipping and squirming between his paws. The twins raced across the beach with it, but just before they reached Clarice, Albert stumbled. The flounder shot out of his paws. Horror-struck, the twins watched it fly through the air and disappear down the back of Clarice's dress.

Clarice screamed and shot into the air. "You little beasts!" she sobbed, jumping up and down to get rid of the horrible slimy fish.

"We're terribly sorry, Clarice," the twins said together.

"That was a disaster," sighed Albert. "We're in trouble now!"

The afternoon ended with a scolding from Mother, and an early bedtime. No hope of getting new fishing rods now!

The next day, the twins tried very hard to make it up to Clarice:

Albert took her breakfast in bed, but whoops!

Then Albertine tried to clear up . . .

Albert thought she might like something nice in her bath . . .

Then Albertine thought some flowers would do the trick . . .

By the end of the day Clarice was more furious with them than she had been before.

"Oh dear," said Albert. "She's even more miserable now."

"Well," replied Albertine, "we'll just have to think of something stupendous, or there'll be no more trips to the beach for us!"

Later on, the twins were playing by the kitchen when they overheard Lily talking to Cook.

"Just think," she was saying, "the Prince of Munster staying here, in St Ivel."

"Ooo, yes," replied Cook. "And I've heard he takes a rowing boat out every day, at three o'clock."

Albert and Albertine stopped dead in their tracks. They both had the very same idea at the same time.

"That's it!" cried Albert. "Clarice needs a prince to rescue her. That would cheer her up."

"But Clarice doesn't need rescuing," said Albertine.

"We can fix that easily," replied Albert. And another plan was born.

Next morning, the twins were especially polite to Clarice. Albert remarked that she was looking very pretty, and Albertine said the sea air must be doing her good.

Then Albert managed to bring her a cup of tea, without spilling it. Clarice seemed pleased, and when the twins proposed an outing in a rowing boat, she agreed to go with them.

They reached the jetty at five to three. The twins were anxiously looking round for the royal mouse when they heard someone calling, "Prince! Prince!" Turning round they saw a smart young mouse in a blue jacket strolling towards them, a spotty dog gambolling at his heels.

"That must be the prince!" whispered Albertine. "Quick, let's put our plan into action."

Albert helped Clarice into the boat and she arranged her skirts on the seat. Then Albertine said, "What's that on the end of your nose, Clarice? Is it a spot?"

"Oh, no. Not another," groaned Clarice, opening her bag to look in her mirror.

Quickly, Albert pushed the boat out with his foot. It drifted away, gently at first, but suddenly the current caught it. The twins held their breath as it sped faster and faster out to sea. All of a sudden Clarice let out the loudest and most terrifying scream the twins had ever heard.

It was all they needed. They raced towards the smart-looking mouse crying, "Help! Help! Our sister's in danger!"

The mouse stared at them in dismay. "I can't swim!" he wailed.

"Oh, no!" groaned Albert. "We've done it again!"

"I'll go and get help," the mouse cried, running off down the beach.

"Prince! Prince!" he called out, and the spotty dog galloped after him.

"Oh, jumping jellyfish," groaned Albert. "Prince is his *dog*."

"What are we going to do now?" wailed Albertine. "Clarice could drown."

But they needn't have worried. There was a huge splash as someone dived off the jetty, and a few minutes later they saw a swimmer reach Clarice and start pulling the boat towards the shore. A big crowd had gathered on the beach as the rescuer carried Clarice onto the sand.

Suddenly, an elderly mouse broke through the crowd and rushed up to the rescuer. Bowing low, he said, "Well done, your Highness!"

"Just wait until Mother hears about this," snarled Clarice, through clenched teeth.

The next day, the twins were strictly forbidden to leave the house. They were sitting miserably in the corner playing noughts and crosses when the doorbell rang and Lily ushered a visitor into the room.

The twins could hardly believe their eyes: it was the prince.

The prince presented Mother with a box of chocolates and then, "For your beautiful daughter," he said, handing Clarice an enormous bunch of flowers. Turning to the twins he gave each of them a long package. Inside were two brand new gleaming fishing rods.

"Looks like we've done something right, at last," said Albert.

And even Clarice smiled.

The Great Green Forest

Paul Geraghty

HIGH UP in the great green forest, the sun began to rise. Way down in the deep dark shadows, a treemouse was curling up to sleep.

Creech! Creech! Woop! Woop!
chirped the frogs. The sounds
were screechy, the sounds
were sharp:
Woopoo! Woopoo!
Creech! Creech!

"Stop that noise!"
yelled the treemouse.
"I'm trying to sleep!"

But all she heard was the *Zee-zee-zee-zee!* of a cicada somewhere outside. *Zee-zee-zee-zee!* Then the *Hmmmm* of a humming bird, *Hmmmm* over here and *Hmmmm* over there.

"Stop that noise!" yelled the treemouse.

"I'm trying to sleep!"

Then *Keeoo . . . kedik-kedik-kedik!* came the calls from the forest crown. Toucans pierced the curtain of green with a *Keeoo . . . kedik-kedik-kedik!*

"Stop that noise!"
yelled the treemouse.
"I'm trying to sleep!"
But the forest was alive
with songs and sounds.

Yaag! Screech-screecha-screecha! squawked a macaw. *Yaag! SCRAAA! SCRAAA!* squawked another.

"Stop that noise!" yelled the treemouse. "I'm trying to sleep!"

But her voice was drowned by the
monkeys that bickered in the branches.
Duwoop! Ooo-ooo-ooo-ooo! whooped one.
Yeek! Yeek! screamed the others.

"Stop that noise!" yelled the treemouse.
"I'm trying to sleep!" And suddenly the
forest fell silent. All she heard was the
echo of her own voice.

Animals clung in silence, not daring to move or make a sound.

Even the cats that ruled the forest now cowered in the quiet. That's better! thought the treemouse.

But it wasn't. She couldn't sleep.
The silence grew worse than any
noise, until finally she cried out,
"Please make some noise!
I'm trying to sleep!"

She waited. And then there was
a noise. She heard a distant *Brrrm,
brrrm . . .* and then a
C-r-r-r-r-r-RACKA-DACKA-RACKA SHOONG!
that shook her to the ground.

A tree had fallen. And a gaping hole was left in the crown of the great green forest.

C-r-r-r-r-r-RACKA-DACKA-RACKA SHOONG!

Another tree came down!

Brrrm, BRRRM . . . an ugly sound made the ground shudder. And the treemouse knew her tree would be next.

She looked up at her home; then she turned to the terrible sound. And at the top of her voice she yelled,

"STOP THAT NOISE!"

But that noise didn't stop.
Brrrm, it drew closer, *BRRRM,* till the
earth thundered; *BRRRM!* till the earth
shook. But the treemouse stood firm.

Then something made the driver stop. And when he stopped, he
felt the silence. He saw the broken trees. He saw the fallen nests.
And he sensed angry eyes watching him.

So he sat and he thought. He stayed there and thought till the sun went down. And when it was dark, he went away.

And he never came back.

Now way up in the great green forest, the trees are growing again.

And deep down in the dark shadows,
a treemouse curls up and closes her
eyes. She listens to the songs and
sounds of the forest, which tell her
that, for now, she can sleep in peace.

Inspector Mouse

Bernard Stone and Ralph Steadman

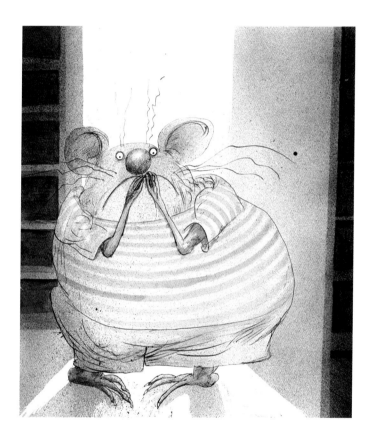

FATTY MOUSE couldn't believe his eyes. He
looked around the store. All the shelves were
empty. There wasn't a piece of cheese in sight.
Someone had found their secret hoard and
stolen it all. This was a case for Inspector Mouse.

Inspector Mouse soon arrived on the scene with his good
friend Toothy Mouse.

"Thank goodness you've come," wailed Fatty Mouse.
"There's been a robbery! Not a morsel of cheese left.
They've taken it all."

"Hmm," said Inspector Mouse, and glanced about the store.
His sharp eyes picked up a clue at once. "Pin-Stripe Mouse," he
muttered.

"How on earth can you tell?" gasped Fatty Mouse, obviously impressed.

"I thought he was on our side," said Toothy, taking out his magnifying glass.

"Never mind, Toothy. Just follow me," replied Inspector Mouse, mysteriously. "*We'll* get to the bottom of it!"

They made their way down to the Danish Blue Cheese Club at the harbour.

The club band, The Roquefours, were playing as they entered the club. Joe Mozzarella Mouse was the drummer. The pianist was Duke Emmental Mouse.

The saxophonist was the famous Camembert Coleman Mouse and the singer was the glamorous Dolcelatte Mouse.

Inspector Mouse strolled over to the bar and turned to face Informer Mouse.

"OK," he said. "Where's Pin-Stripe Mouse?"

Informer Mouse trembled with fear. "Sure – he's – he's down at the old fish warehouse on the waterfront. The gang has a hideout there," he stuttered.

Approaching the gang's hideout, Inspector Mouse and Toothy Mouse crept stealthily into the building.

"They are probably in the basement, Toothy," whispered Inspector Mouse. "Let's have a look through the trap-door."

"You're right," gasped Toothy. "And that's our cheese piled up in the middle. Let's surprise them."

"No, wait," warned Inspector Mouse. "They are all here –
Pin-Stripe Mouse, Parmesan Cheese Mouse, Munster Mouse,
Suntan Mouse, the lovely Betty Brie Mouse and Mr Big himself.
We'll need help."

The gang was listening to the M.B.C. Television News
broadcast.

> *"News-flash! A consignment of Limburger cheese*
> *for the Lord Mayor's Banquet is now on its way*
> *up river, by barge, with a special escort of police mice."*

Mr Big chuckled and his huge shoulders shook with glee.

"That's for us," he said greedily. "It's the dream cheese of every
connoisseur. Let's pay them a surprise visit. It's Limburger cheese
for supper at the club tonight, boys!"

Inspector Mouse turned to Toothy and ordered, "Quick, to
the pier. No time to lose. We will watch and wait."

Meanwhile, the special police escort glided silently up the river.
As they kept a watchful eye on the precious cargo, the police

mice began to feel very drowsy and were soon overcome by the powerful smell of the Limburger cheese.

The gang, wearing special
equipment, had no trouble
at all in stealing the cheese
and escaping.

Inspector Mouse
watched the gang come
ashore and hurry away
to the club.

"Don't worry,
Toothy," he said. "Here
come the police now,
hot on their tails.
Quick, into that old car.
You drive."

They zoomed
off in hot
pursuit, eager
for the chase.

The car spluttered to a halt outside the Danish Blue Cheese Club. Tumbling out of the car they crashed through the door and into the club.

"Stay where you are. This is a raid!" shouted Inspector Mouse. He nodded towards Pin-Stripe Mouse, who opened the drum. There it was! The stolen cheese from the barge.

"Oh no!" cried Joe Mozzarella Mouse. "We've been tricked!"

Toothy was amazed. "So you were on our side after all," he said to Pin-Stripe Mouse.

"Elementary, my dear Toothy. You're right as usual," said Inspector Mouse. "I don't know what I'd do without you. Now why don't you play the piano? What was that song . . ?

"Play it again, Toothy."

Acknowledgements

The publishers gratefully acknowledge the following authors and illustrators:

Town House Mouse published by Hutchinson Children's Books
Published by agreement with Walker & Co., New York
Text and illustrations © Nigel Brooks and Abigail Horner, 1999

Herbert Binns and the Flying Tricycle published by Hutchinson Children's Books
Text © Caroline Castle, 1986 Illustrations © Peter Weevers, 1986

Look Out, Patrick! published by Hutchinson Children's Books
Text and illustrations © Paul Geraghty, 1990

Mouse and Mole published by Doubleday Children's Books
Text © Joyce Dunbar, 1993 Illustrations © James Mayhew, 1993
With thanks to The Agency (London) Ltd

The Tale of Admiral Mouse published by Andersen Press
Text © Bernard Stone, 1981 Illustrations © Tony Ross, 1981

Albert and Albertine at the Seaside published by Hutchinson Children's Books
Text and illustrations © Colin and Moira Maclean, 1989

The Great Green Forest published by Hutchinson Children's Books
Text and illustrations © Paul Geraghty, 1992

Inspector Mouse published by Andersen Press
Text © Bernard Stone, 1980 Illustrations © Ralph Steadman, 1980

With special thanks to Andersen Press
for their generous contribution to this collection

Contents

Introduction

I'm sure even the most experienced gardeners agree that their greatest challenge isn't growing perennials from seed or getting the garden to bloom from May to October. It's planning the garden in the first place. Because a true garden isn't just a collection of beautiful flowers — it's a useable space meant for people, with places for activities and storage as well as plants.

When I started gardening, I wanted space for the barbecue and clothesline as well as my dreamed-of perennial beds, but I didn't know where to begin. So I started with an island bed near the sliding doors to the house. It looked like a flower-covered grave, and was exactly where we wanted to sit when a beautiful day beckoned us outdoors. The rest of the yard

was a disconnected wasteland — the sandbox in one corner, the clothesline in another, the barbecue wherever we happened to be.

It took me two years to realize that planning a successful garden is really a matter of organization, of allowing form to follow function. We moved the sandbox under the apple tree where the kids played anyway, and replaced the unfortunate flower bed with a patio. The clothesline was hidden in a lattice enclosure which also provided storage for the tricycles and the barbecue.

Canadian Gardening's Creating a Garden is designed to make it easy for both neophyte and experienced gardeners to have the garden of their dreams. From the step-by-step description of what's involved in creating a garden to the lushly photographed features on today's most popular garden styles, you'll find a wealth of practical information and great ideas you'll refer to again and again as your garden evolves.

Liz Primeau, Editor,
Canadian Gardening Magazine

CHAPTER ONE

SETTING *the* STAGE

"In the arrangement of any site, the natural conditions of the place should be studied. If they are emphatic, or in any way distinct, they should be carefully maintained and fostered. It is grievous to see, in a place that has some well-defined natural character, that character destroyed or stultified, for it is just that quality that is the most precious."

— Gertrude Jekyll

Getting Started

Whenever we step into a wonderful garden, we're struck by how *right* it feels. Everything seems to come together, and there is nothing awkward or out-of-place in the setting. But when it comes to planning our own garden, most of us feel incompetent. We may know what we want — but we have no idea how to put it all together, let alone make it soar. Discouraged, we abandon all attempts at composition and plunge in headfirst. We cut flower beds into the lawn, buy a few plants and soon we can't imagine things any other way. The vision is lost, never to be found again.

While it may take a lifetime to master the art, it *is* possible for anyone to develop a good working knowledge of garden design. By approaching the planning process as a series of uncomplicated steps and by following simple rules, the novice designer can come satisfyingly close to gardening perfection.

STEP I

RECORD *the* EXISTING CONDITIONS

Happily, you don't have to design in a vacuum. There is a mass of information out in your garden that will help establish the broad strokes of your design. The first task is to understand and record the existing conditions, to build up a picture of what is where. Remember that in the early stages of the design agenda you must think in general, or conceptual, terms; only at the end of the process will you flesh out and refine the details.

On a large piece of graph paper, draw a scale diagram of the garden. Let 1/4 inch or 1/2 inch (2 cm or 4 cm) on paper represent 1 foot (1 m) on site. With the house as your baseline, work outward to measure and mark down the garden's boundaries and most important features — permanent structures such as a garage, fences, walls; trees and other major plantings; level changes, entry and exit points. Indicate the location of the main rooms, windows and doors. Show overhead wires and buried gas, electrical and water lines (local utilities will provide this information); in front gardens, take note of the boulevard allowances (the part of the property the city or township controls). Show outdoor faucets and power outlets; indicate the garden's orientation to north.

Even the smallest details play a part in the overall design of a garden. A basketful of violas (above), spilling over a stone urn, makes a charming accent in a country garden.

Collecting and setting down this basic site information will greatly help you grasp the nature of the space you're dealing with and give you a pretty good idea what changes will, or will not, be possible. If you really cannot face doing a scale plan, or if your property is too large for you to manage alone, seek help. A student of architecture, landscape architecture or interior design would welcome the work at a modest fee.

STEP 2

UNDERSTAND *the* GARDEN YOU HAVE

Once your plan is prepared, your next task is to understand and record the garden's strengths and weaknesses — a process professionals call site analysis. With a list of simple questions in hand, take a long, critical look from inside the house and from various points in the garden. If possible, do this over a year since gardens change so much from season to season.

Is there a pleasant view you might highlight or an unpleasant one you would prefer to lose? Are there trees or other nice features outside the garden you might visually borrow? Are some areas private and others not? Will measures be needed to improve light or drainage? Watch for sun and shade at different times of day and through the year, and for wet or dry spots — these factors will dictate where and how you plant the garden.

Using an overlay of tracing paper, add the information you have collected to your master plan. This process further helps you understand your garden, but, more important, it begins to tell you how your design must be organized.

❧ Paths will obviously start from doors and gates (but not from windows) and they will go somewhere — to a utility area or seating spot and not to a dead end at the fence line.

❧ Planting spaces must be in sun or shade, as appropriate — you won't plan a rose bed in the dense shade of a large maple, or a woodland garden in a dry, sunny spot.

❧ A dining area will go close to the house and where there is some degree of privacy — not where you must make a long trek with every dish and glass, or under your neighbor's kitchen window. If you have a privacy problem, plan a way to solve it.

All this may seem very obvious but, in fact, most home gardeners do *not* recognize the value of working from what you know. Professional designers do and that's why professionally designed gardens feel right and work well. The garden plan grows out of the natural conditions and layout of the site; it accentuates the positive and plays down the negative. Working from what you know speeds the novice through the basic design process in a series of easy-to-handle steps.

SITE ANALYSIS — *The* QUESTIONS *to* ASK

❧ Which areas are sunny or shady — when and for how long?

❧ Are some areas too wet or too dry?

❧ Are strong winds a problem — and if so, where?

❧ Where is privacy good? Where does it need to be improved?

❧ Is security, access or safety a problem?

❧ What about noise from the street or from neighbors?

❧ Have natural patterns of use and movement already been established in the garden — are there places you always sit? Do you habitually take one route from A to B?

❧ Is there an obvious spot for a utility area for composting and storage — somewhere that's convenient, but unobtrusive? Will it need to be camouflaged with a screen or hedge?

❧ Where are good views? What can be done to improve poor ones?

❧ Are there features to be visually borrowed from outside the garden?

❧ Which existing trees, shrubs or plantings would you like to keep in your new garden?

❧ What about your soil — is it heavy clay or sandy, and what is its pH?

In order to make the best use of the space you have, your garden should be designed with your needs and your lifestyle in mind.

STEP 3

THINK *of the* GARDEN YOU WOULD LIKE

Now that you know a lot about your garden, it's time to get to know about yourself. Thinking about yourself, your family, your needs and lifestyle will help you develop a wish list detailing what you want or need in your garden.

Perhaps you are a single, working person who will use the garden mainly for evening entertaining — you might plan a simple space for outdoor cooking and dining, with low-maintenance planting and night lighting. Perhaps you have a young family with the need for lots of play space, good visibility from house to garden and masses of storage. Or perhaps you are retired and look forward to some serious flower and vegetable gardening.

Your interests and daily routine are relevant, too. Are you a collector of *objets* — art, sculpture, pots or just plain junk? Are you an avid plants person with a special passion for herbs, alpines or roses? Do you love to read or sew, or do you spend half the day on the phone, laptop or ironing? All these interests and activities can be planned into your garden. And you may have a particular fancy for your garden — a pool or pond, running water, a gazebo, a hammock — or a particular need such as wheelchair, stroller or bicycle access, or a dog run.

On a new overlay of tracing paper, begin to rough in the major elements from your wish list — from swimming pool to laundry line. Think only in broad terms; the detail comes later. All the things you already know about the garden will help you decide where best to locate each feature. By defining and limiting your wish list early in the planning process, you will be able to build your design around it. Form will develop from function. Be realistic and accept that you may have to make choices. Remember, too, that it's best to do a few things well.

STEP 4

ESTABLISH A FRAMEWORK

The steps so far involve easy-to-know elements. They're all there in your garden, in your life, and you simply collect and sort them. The next step may be a little more challenging because it's unfamiliar. You are now ready to establish a framework — to add the linear and directional information that will shape your design and bring it together in an effective way.

Using tracing paper over the master plan and a bright-colored pencil, extend lines out from the house, its windows and doors, and from other significant points in the garden (gates, garden buildings, etc.). These lines will establish the plan's orientation and major axes. Add lines at 45° and 90° angles to the main axes to form a grid which will help you define and separate spaces in the garden and suggest ways to change direction coherently within the design.

Don't get too tense about this. Throw down the lines and see what they tell you about the geometry of your space. Use them as the frame upon which to hang and connect the main elements of your design (terrace, path, steps, planting areas) and to help you line things up — focal points from gates or windows, the edge of a path with the corner of the house. Using a framework makes a garden scheme much more coherent.

The first four steps — recording the existing conditions, getting to know your garden, developing your wish list and establishing a framework — form the bones of a garden that will prove practical and structurally well-founded. Your garden should work as efficiently as a well-designed kitchen, without hindrance or irrelevant detail; it should connect to and flow from the house in a logical way. While good design never shouts contrivance, it is always quietly present when we have a sense of rightness in a space.

STEP 5

DEVELOP A GARDEN STYLE

Gardeners through history have hotly debated the issue of garden style. Is a garden by definition something made, and apart from nature, or should it replicate nature as far as possible? And how far *is* possible? For most of us, this comes down to settling on a look or feel for our garden.

First, consult the *genius loci* — the spirit of the place. Try to understand the special character of your garden. Is it essentially urban or rural, intimate or open? What about the architecture of your house: is it modern or traditional, angular or curved, horizontal or vertical? Study the neighborhood streetscape and note the trees and other plants growing locally. Garden and setting are partners, each potentially enhancing or diminishing the other, so take your cue from the spirit of the place and use it to inform your design approach.

Turn to other people's gardens, books and magazines for inspiration. Look, record, work out how and why things work and why you like them. (Feel no guilt at this — creative borrowing is at the heart of gardening history!) It is important, though, not to lift ideas pell-mell; rather, use them to generate your own style, to create your own harmonies.

In developing a garden style, aim to settle on an image or look that is compatible with the garden's setting and the local vernacular — and expressive of your own tastes. Then stick with it. Use only ideas that work with your style; discard those that do not. Remember that while harmony is quietly acknowledged in a well-designed garden, its absence is painfully obvious.

In any garden, a successful planting scheme combines and contrasts the form and color of both flowers and foliage.

STEP 6

STRIKE A COMFORTABLE BALANCE

Form, balance, scale and contrast are central to good design indoors and out. In the garden, we aim for a comfortable balance between mass and void, between the design choices that add bulk (such as structures, trees, major plantings) and those that contribute open spaces (such as paving, grass and water). We play with height and weight, light and shade to achieve a sense of equilibrium, or we juxtapose them to achieve specific effects.

Talk of form and balance may induce panic, but there are good practical ways to achieve them, both at the drafting stage and later outside in the garden. You can try your ideas out by sketching them onto a photographic image of your garden. Connect photographs together to create a whole vista of the garden, enlarge the image on a photocopier and very broadly superimpose the main features of your proposed design. Are the proportions right? Does the scheme feel well balanced?

You can confirm a good fit right in the garden by mapping the design out with stakes and string or a chalk line. Plot paved areas, paths and steps, rough-in planting areas, locate fencing, hedges, structures and ornamental features. Use sturdy stakes for trees. View the results from all perspectives and tinker as necessary. You'll be surprised to discover how sure you'll be when you hit it right.

STEP 7

UNDERSTAND *the* PRINCIPLES *of* PLANTING

Plants are an integral part of the garden's architecture. They should be chosen primarily, though not solely, for their structural and textural qualities and for the role they will play in your design. You might, for example, use plants as a focal point, to frame a view or to mark an entry or transition point in the garden. They can also be employed to create a privacy screen, to blur a boundary line or to play with perspective.

As you add plants to your plan, think first in very general terms, identifying the need for something tall and upright here, low and spreading there, something light and airy or dense and shiny. Start with trees, which are the strongest vertical elements in a planting scheme, and work down through shrubs (which add bulk) to perennials and ground covers. Rough your ideas onto your plan using a circle template to help you match the size of the plant with the amount of space you have available. Make specific plant choices only when you feel comfortable with the broad scheme.

It's important to understand the individual character of each plant you choose, so spend time at plant nurseries and with a good plant dictionary. As most things bloom for only part of the season, be sure you look at a plant's other qualities — its leaves, bark, branch structure, fruiting and so on — and try to chose things that have more than one brief, wonderful moment. Be sure that you also understand the cultural needs of plants and their mature size — which may be much larger than you would like!

In developing the fine detail of your planting scheme, combine and contrast the form and color of both flowers and foliage, plan for a sequence of bloom from early spring to late fall and give thought to winter interest. For example, evergreens should be distributed equally through the garden as they are denser than most deciduous plants and stand out starkly after the leaves have fallen. Plant smaller things in masses for bold effect and try to limit your choices to a small, unified palette.

While many things about gardening are truly in the lap of the gods, design need not be one of them. Thoughtful observation and planning, along with a clear reading of the setting and the subordination of detail to a dominant idea, will result in a garden that's a pleasure to look at and to be in — in short, an enduring delight.

GARDEN ELEMENTS

Hard Elements

❧ Buildings: summer-houses, gazebos, storage sheds.

❧ Fencing, with or without gate (closed for privacy, or open trellis for site division): wire, timber, bamboo, iron.

❧ Walls to retain level changes: brick, stone, concrete, block and stucco, timber.

❧ Walls for site division and privacy: brick, stone, concrete, block and stucco.

❧ Paving materials for terraces, pathways, steps: brick, flagstone, granite cobblestones, concrete (poured or pavers), asphalt, gravel.

❧ Ornamental structures: arches, arbors, pergolas, covered seats, obelisks.

❧ Water: pond or fountain.

❧ Lighting (ornamental or security): low-voltage or standard.

Soft Elements

❧ Vines: evergreen or deciduous, self-clinging or twining.

❧ Annuals and biennials.

❧ Perennials.

❧ Bulbs: spring and summer blooming.

❧ Trees and Shrubs: large or small, evergreen or deciduous.

❧ Hedges: evergreen or deciduous.

Decorative Elements

❧ Sculpture: traditional or modern.

❧ Furniture: for informal seating, dining or working.

❧ Containers: traditional or modern.

CHAPTER TWO

GARDEN STYLES

*The look, or style,
of a garden depends as much on the existing
setting as it does on the owner's tastes.
If you take your cue from the spirit of the place,
you'll discover how easy it is to create the
garden you've always wanted — whether it's
a sophisticated urban oasis, a tranquil Japanese-
inspired retreat or an old-fashioned cottage
garden spilling over with riotous blooms.*

The COTTAGE GARDEN

The delicate white flowers and striking foliage of Clematis armandii *embroider a whimsical cottage-garden fence.*

HISTORY

The first cottage gardens were born of necessity, not style. They were the gardens of farm workers and other laborers who had families to feed and used the bit of land around their cottages to grow what they could. Much later, garden designers imitated the style and elevated the humble cottage garden to the status of high fashion.

In today's world, the cottage-style garden is much admired, although more for its lush tumble of flowers than for the vegetables, chickens and goats that marked its original incarnation. Cottage gardens were honest gardens, made to please the family and to supply what it needed. Because they were so crowded, crop rotation was a necessity; manure and other organic composts were used freely, and the garden was always alive with bees, butterflies and other beneficial insects. Although the appeal of the cottage garden today is mostly esthetic, its good garden practices are well worth emulating.

The cottage-garden look: (clockwise from left)
a simple white picket fence and a tumble of delphiniums,
old-fashioned roses and poppies; a twig arch framing a wood-chip
path; a garden chair fashioned of willow twigs.

STRUCTURE AND DESIGN

The cottage garden is, by definition, small, making it ideal for a city or suburban lot. But the style is still possible in a larger space — simply cordon off an area and fence it with pickets or a screen of woven willow.

❦ Inside its precincts, an eclectic jumble of plants includes flowers for cutting intermixed with vegetables for the table. A cottage garden may look overgrown, but it's never left to run riot — at its heart, there is a plan.

❦ A strong framework of beds and pathways provides the structure, with the pathways always leading somewhere — straight to the front door, to a small seating area with a pond, to the herb garden and the compost heap. But materials are informal: gravel or limestone screenings, old brick, randomly laid stone, even earth or bark chips.

❦ Statuary, of the classical or garden-gnome variety, is nonexistent; it was beyond the means of the cottage gardener of a century or two ago. An arbor or bench, made of wood or willow twigs rather than expensive cast iron, is most appropriate as a focal point. Another cottage feature is the gate; originally used to keep the cows out, today it provides authentic cottage-style detail.

GETTING THE LOOK

❦ **Forget grass:** Cottage gardens were chock-full of flowers, vegetables, herbs and fruits, with planting areas divided by pathways.

❦ **Use natural materials:** Pathways should be gravel, flat stone or older brick, never modern concrete pavers. Edge with river pebbles, sea shells, shingles or a low, trimmed boxwood hedge.

❦ **Fence it in:** Use low weathered pickets, peeled poles, woven willow, split cedar post-and-rail construction, or a brick or stone wall.

❦ **Use simple outdoor furniture:** Wood or worn metal works best; white resin or plastic and modern loungers spoil the effect. An old kitchen table allowed to weather is ideal.

❧ **Use everything and anything as plant containers:** Barrels, old tin cans, wood-stave fruit baskets and clay pots.

❧ **Edge beds with vegetables:** Frilly leaf lettuce or curly parsley are especially striking.

❧ **Let it spread:** Allow ground covers and low herbs, such as thyme, to sprout between paving stones or in gravel paths.

❧ **Keep it small:** Cottage gardens were small because properties weren't large. If you live in the country, divide your cottage garden from the larger acreage with a low stone wall so you can "borrow" the view of fields and woods beyond it.

PLANTING

Cottage gardeners didn't have access to garden centers and unlimited varieties of flowers — they depended on wildflowers and cuttings from their neighbors. Today's cottage garden should be planted with old-fashioned varieties of perennials and annuals.

❧ For spring, plant large drifts of crocus and daffodils among the perennials.

❧ Allow annuals like cosmos, nicotiana and poppies to self-seed at will, thinning them out where they're too crowded to mature or where they're choking out other plants.

❧ Try the "dot" approach to planting: instead of banking plants from low to high, set one or two tall plants, such as hollyhocks or sunflowers, among large drifts of medium or low ones, or plant a single specimen at the edge of the pathway.

❧ To keep the overall mood informal, allow sprawling plants or vines such as ivy and nasturtium to tumble over the edges of the pathways.

❧ Balance a bed of mixed colors with some white or grey plants, like oxeye daisies, furry lamb's-ears or artemisia.

Although cottage gardens are crowded and informal, they are not maintenance-free. They require constant dead-heading (the removal of spent flower heads) to keep annuals blooming. Overgrown clumps of perennials have to be split and plants staked. Stakes should be simple — sturdy twigs placed in a crossover pattern in the ground to support a sprawling plant; a branched twig set in the middle of a plant; wood or bamboo poles. A tepee of poles tied with twine makes an effective and attractive support for scarlet runner beans or morning glory.

A tumble of flowers, especially fragrant old-fashioned roses, are the signature of a cottage garden. (Clockwise from top left) Yellow roses and purple foxglove, with geraniums in a terra-cotta pot; white peonies, pink roses (Rosa 'Bonica') and grey lamb's-ears (Stachys byzantina); more roses, blue lace-cap hydrangea and the mauve flowers of Buddleia davidii.

SELECTED PLANTS

❧ PERENNIALS: Phlox, daylilies, pinks, lady's-mantle, delphiniums, violas, lavender and other herbs, mallow, foxglove, lupines, bleeding heart, lilies, old rose species, lily-of-the-valley.

❧ CLIMBERS: Scarlet runner bean, sweet peas, old climbing roses, wild cucumber, Dutchman's-pipe, ornamental gourds.

❧ ANNUALS AND BIENNIALS: Cosmos, nicotiana, verbascum, forget-me-nots, sweet alyssum, sunflowers, hollyhocks, poppies, nigella, oxeye daisies, wallflowers, cornflowers.

❧ SPRING BULBS: Tulips, particularly the older, clearer-colored types; daffodils; grape hyacinths; species crocus.

The FORMAL GARDEN

HISTORY

The secret of an attractive garden, whatever its style, lies in the pleasing arrangement of its various elements — plants, paths, structures and ornaments. In a formal garden, this arrangement is geometric, with elements arranged in distinct patterns, while an informal garden is asymmetrical, with a soft, subtle, natural look.

The Egyptian gardens of 1400 B.C. are among the earliest examples of a formal garden style. This style reached its apogee in the eighteenth century during the Enlightenment, which emphasized geometry, balance and symmetry. During this period, formal gardens were seen as a physical manifestation of the belief in the essentially rational nature of the universe. The style flourished throughout Europe, particularly in France, where the gardens at Versailles remain as the most outstanding example of formal garden design. With the rise of the Landscape movement in England, however, a formal approach to garden design was replaced by a more natural style. Today, homeowners with small gardens or traditional houses favor a formal garden style.

Set against a backdrop of manicured cedar hedges, an elegant statue serves as a focal point in a contemporary formal garden. A lush planting of variegated hostas anchors the statue in the setting.

STRUCTURE *and* DESIGN

In all gardens, there is a play between the imposed pattern of the garden — the location of stairs and terraces, the layout and construction of the paths, the size of the beds — and the plants that grow and change with the seasons. In formal gardens, the imposed pattern has the upper hand, and the plants fall under its control, often functioning as a living extension of the design. To maintain the controlled look, formal gardens are usually enclosed with hedges, walls or fences.

❦ The essential building blocks of a formal garden design are balance, proportion and symmetry. Put simply, that means thinking in terms of squares, triangles, circles, hexagons and other geometric shapes arranged in orderly patterns.

❦ Often, one half of the garden is a mirror reflection of the other half. For example, a perennial border edged in trimmed boxwood would be sited opposite one with the same dimensions and plants, arranged in precisely the same way. An asymmetrical detail in a formal garden is the exception, but often works because it creates a contrast that reinforces the overall design.

An ornate round stone basin (above), surrounded by a well-groomed edging of ground cover, lends an air of antiquity to this formal garden. Curving gravel paths and circular flower beds, planted in a repeating pattern, echo the dominant shape of the ornamental basin and draw the eye to it.

❧ Paths in formal gardens are generally straight and meet other paths at right angles; common materials are brick or square-cut stone. An urn on either side of a set of steps adds balance.

❧ Vistas in a formal garden are created by the overall design of the garden, and lead the eye to a focal point such as a birdbath, statue or sundial. In a large formal garden, an allée of trees leading to a fountain or bench serves a similar purpose. For greater effect, a garden ornament is often centered at the end of a wrought-iron archway planted with matching climbing roses or ivy on either side.

❧ Formal gardens rely on structures more than other styles do. Gazebos, pavilions, arches, pergolas, bowers and arbors made from traditional materials are common features. Fences are usually wood, brick or stone; gates are ornamental yet functional. Steps, stairs, and ornaments are often made of stone or moulded concrete.

❧ Water is often a feature of a formal garden — a round or square reflecting pool edged with stone, or a fountain with splashing water. Appropriate furniture in a formal garden includes stone benches or a cast-iron table and chairs. White resin chaise longues and Adirondack chairs are too casual.

SELECTED PLANTS

All plants in a formal garden are carefully chosen for shape and color, and beds are kept well-groomed to enhance the overall design.

❧ Although masses of flowers are planted in geometrical beds with finely defined edges, a variety of colors and textures saves a formal design from monotony.

❧ A strong formal effect can be created by filling four small symmetrical beds with precisely the same plants — for example, a star magnolia, dusty miller and variegated oat grass. Or, use flowers of similar colors, such as all-white blooms, or plants with leaves of a similar hue.

❧ Tightly packed beds of ornamental kale, planted in rows of contrasting colors, look striking in a formal garden in the fall.

❧ Plants with architectural qualities, such as yucca, verbascums and dracaena spikes, are particularly effective when placed at regular intervals in the garden.

❧ Use annuals in contrasting colors — such as dwarf or fern-leaf marigold with red celosia — to make a sharp-edged pattern in a formal flower bed. Nicotiana, sanvitalia and rudbeckia are other excellent choices. Hummocks of moss phlox (*P. subulata*) in contrasting colors make a pleasing spring picture, but they'll need to be pruned after blooming to keep them tidy and within bounds.

❧ To edge borders, elegant lady's mantle (*Alchemilla mollis*) and hostas are a hardy alternative for areas where winters are too cold for boxwood.

❧ Precisely trimmed hedging is another feature of a formal garden. Yew works well, and can either be trimmed into globes or carefully trained to create an arched doorway. Juniper, euonymus and ivy are suitable evergreens to work with, too. One particularly effective way to use statuary in a formal garden is to tuck it into a recess in the hedge. Boxwood and yew can also be planted singly or in groups in a large container and trimmed into fanciful shapes.

Elements that are mirror images of each other abound in a formal garden and underscore the concern with balance, proportion and symmetry that is at the heart of this classical garden style.

The JAPANESE GARDEN

*A basin set on a grouping of rocks (tsukubai) is
common outside ceremonial sites in Japan, and is used by visitors
for washing hands before entering a sacred place.*

HISTORY

The Japanese garden is a landscape in
miniature. Its rocks represent
mountains; a small waterfall and stream
are the mighty cascade and river rushing
to meet the plain — which is, in reality, a
bed of moss planted with a few pines
carefully pruned to look aged and
windswept. Perhaps the river is not water
at all, but is etched with pebbles that
empty into a "sea" of sand raked in the
pattern of waves.

This doesn't mean the gardener has
imitated nature. Instead, he has distilled
its essence in order to create a garden that
symbolizes nature. This may seem a fine
point, but it's a concept integral to the
design of Japanese gardens. The gardener
has followed the principles of *in* and *yo*
(better known by their Chinese names, *yin*

and *yang*) so that everything in the garden
is balanced with its opposite — mass
with space, dark with light, vertical with
horizontal.

As in nature, nothing is symmetrical:
paths wander and ponds are irregular.
Trees are artfully placed to frame a view
and, as in art, areas of empty space are
left to rest the eye and accent the
composition. Indeed, nature has for
centuries been woven into the fabric of
Japanese art, architecture and poetry as
well as into its gardens. Man-made
miniature mountains and lakes were used
as far back as the seventh century, and a
discussion of the placement and grouping
of rocks was part of an eleventh-century
treatise on gardening, the world's earliest
known handbook on garden design. Zen
philosophies and the tea ceremony have
also influenced Japanese gardens because

they are part of the country's culture and values, and appropriate to family and home.

These principles should not daunt the Canadian gardener, however, because Japanese gardens are eminently suited to our modern lifestyle. They require only a little maintenance on a regular basis; they have an atmosphere of calm and peace; and they're well-suited to small or difficult spaces — such as the postage-stamp backyard of an urban townhouse or tiny basement walkout, or a narrow shaded area between buildings, where a dry stone creek bed and a lantern with a growth of moss can offer a solution to a sunless space.

Small areas like these are easier to design than large ones (which don't often exist in Japan), but a corner of a large property can be turned into a small meditative oasis, with a stone bench, a winding path and some subtle greenery. Be sure, though, to divide it from the rest of the garden with a fence or hedge.

MAKING A
JAPANESE-STYLE GARDEN

❧ The cardinal rule: keep it simple. Japanese gardens are never filled with riotous color or a lot of detail. They are designed to be seen from the house, as an extension of it, and materials that harmonize with the house are most appropriate.

❧ A feeling of depth is also essential. Contrary to western garden design, a large tree such as a pine or maple is often planted near the house, with its limbs pruned to frame the view. Smaller trees are planted in the background to give the feeling of distance. Using the same principle, shrubs with large leaves are placed in the foreground and smaller-leaved shrubs behind them. Paths and streams that wind out of sight, perhaps into a small "woodland" of straight trees set in a bed of mounding ground covers, have the same effect.

❧ Curving pathways of small flat stepping stones, set on grass, moss or a wide bed of fine gravel, are used to connect the parts of the garden. Stones are selected with care to harmonize with one another, and they're usually placed close together to make the observer slow down and appreciate the surroundings. Low-lying ferns or junipers work well as borders on the gravel pathways, and the gravel also functions as a mulch. A low Japanese lantern, made of stone or well-weathered concrete, or a single large rock or group of rocks

The serenity of a Japanese garden invites quiet meditation. Soothing green is the predominant color, and weathered wood or stone enhances the carefully positioned plantings of small trees, shrubs and ornamental grasses.

make pleasing ornaments alongside the path.

❧ Japanese gardeners dedicate a lot of time and energy to the selection and placement of rocks, choosing ones in subdued colors and digging them in firmly to give the impression the rocks have always been there. Benches or bridges constructed out of flat rocks are also used.

❧ Water is a common feature in Japanese gardens — quietly murmuring in a stream, splashing over a waterfall, lying passively in a stone basin or trickling into it from a bamboo pipe (a *kakei*) in which is hidden a plastic tube connected to a water source.

Japanese gardens are monochromatic, by western standards. Green is the dominant color, and plants are grouped to show off their different tones and textures. Other colors reflect the changing seasons — the spring blooms of a cherry or crab apple tree, azaleas and rhododendrons in summer, and the fall colors of maples.

GETTING *the* LOOK

Rocks are important styling details. When making a rock composition, group a tall, monolithic shape with a low, mounding stone and perhaps a small flat stone. Surround with a ground cover. Or group three or five craggy, flat-topped stones in a bed of sand; thinking of it as a cluster of mountains rising out of the sea will help create the tableau. Rake the sand to represent waves.

Use stained, not painted, decking and fencing. Raised plank pathways look good traversing a pond or a low area of the garden planted with ferns and ground covers.

Make seats of stone slabs or wood planks set on stacked stones and keep them low. Always select simple garden furniture made of natural materials.

❧ If you don't have space for a natural pond (and ponds should never look man-made or be perfectly round or square), a small water detail is equally effective. Use a terra-cotta pot or purchased stone basin (*chozu-bachi*). Small stone basins were used in the tea garden to wash one's hands before the tea ceremony, and a small bamboo dipper was set on its edge.

❧ Make fences of bamboo or wooden poles set vertically or in a wide lattice pattern, supported by strong wooden posts and lashed together with twine.

❧ Split-bamboo blinds make good patio screens or warm-weather dividers within the garden.

❧ When placing stepping stones, set long ones horizontally across the path, and bury them almost to their surface in the soil; never sit them on top.

❧ Use ornaments sparingly, and try to make them functional as well as attractive — a working stone lantern at the curve of a path, for example. One focal point in a small garden is quite sufficient.

❧ Prune small trees, such as Japanese maple, to resemble large shade trees — maintain a single trunk and thin out branches, keeping foliage toward the end of the branches. Dwarf crab apples can be trained to look gnarled and pines to look windswept; protecting tree limbs with a pad of cloth, use stakes and wire to bend the young limbs into the desired position.

SELECTED PLANTS

❧ SHRUBS AND LOW EVERGREENS: Burning bush (*Euonymus alata*) has red foliage in fall and attractive winter bark. Oregon holly (*Mahonia aquifolium*) is good in the winter garden. *Hydrangea paniculata* and *H. quercifolia* offer texture and bloom. Rhododendrons and azalea are classically Japanese, and there are many varieties. White forsythia (*Abeliophyllum distichum*) has early spring blossoms. Creeping juniper (*Juniperus horizontalis*), mugo pine (*Pinus mugo*), wintergreen (*Gaultheria procumbens*), Japanese spurge (*Pachysandra terminalis*) and periwinkle (*Vinca minor*) are excellent ground covers, as are ivies (*Hedera helix*) and wintercreeper (*Euonymus fortunei*) in its many forms.

Although a Japanese garden is monochromatic, seasonal flowers provide contrasting color. A spectacular magnolia tree (right), in full bloom, frames a tall garden gate; delicate pink waterlilies (above) enhance the beauty and serenity of a garden pond.

❧ TREES: Small to medium types work best — crab apple (*Malus* spp.), honey locust (*Gleditsia* spp.), mountain ash (*Sorbus* spp.) and Japanese maple (*Acer palmatum*), which comes in many varieties, some with green foliage and some with subdued red. Also, members of the *Prunus* family, such as cherry, flowering almond and plum. Magnolia, birch (*Betula*), willow (*Salix* spp.) and pines are also effective.

❧ HEDGES AND VINES: A cedar hedge around the garden is a striking way to define and enclose the space. Firethorn (*Pyracantha coccinea*) and bittersweet (*Celastrus scandens*) are both fine climbers with winter berries; firethorn also keeps its leaves in winter. Wisteria is another vine popular in Japan.

❧ PERENNIALS: Siberian and Japanese iris provide subtle hints of color, and both flowers and foliage suit the style. Peonies in muted colors are also appropriate, as are many perennial cranesbill (*Geranium*). Ornamental grasses of all kinds complement evergreens; low ones like sheep's fescue (*Festuca glauca*), planted in mass, can double as miniature shrubs in a Japanese "landscape" — as can ferns, especially Japanese painted fern (*Athyrium nipponicum* 'Pictum'), and all kinds of hosta. If you have a pond, be sure to include waterlilies.

GARDENS *in a* MEDITERRANEAN STYLE

Mediterranean gardens — and their precursors, the gardens of the Moors and Persians — were created to offer shelter from a climate characterized by hot, dry days under a beating sun and warm, moist nights. And as anyone who has visited the area knows, Mediterranean gardens — and those of Southern California and Southern Australia, which share a similar climate — invite relaxation, enjoyment and civilized behavior.

Mediterranean courtyards and terraces are filled with color that comes from structures, pots and tiles as much as from plants. In fact, most plants are dormant in summer because of the hot weather, making fall and spring the main growing seasons. Vine-covered pergolas offer protection from the sun's rays, a large table is available for family dinners alfresco, and the fragrance of

herbs, citrus and cypress fills the air.

Creating a Mediterranean-style garden in Canada may seem an impossible stretch for many people, but it's really a matter of capturing the style. The secret is to study the structural and horticultural features of a Mediterranean garden, then adapt them to suit your location.

❧ Most Mediterranean gardens are smallish and enclosed, making the style ideal for urban settings, or for a corner of a large garden.

❧ Because lawns can't stand the summer heat, they are nearly non-existent in the Mediterranean; instead, courtyards are surfaced in gravel or random paving stones — both popular and climate-hardy materials here — and surrounded by a bit of grass or herbs.

❧ Many Mediterranean plants grow here, too — including santolina, wisteria, viburnum, juniper, pines, lilies, lilacs and most herbs.

A sophisticated garden in the heart of Toronto (right) offers a contemporary interpretation of the Mediterranean style. A rough-hewn wooden table invites entertainment and relaxation while, overhead, a canopy of foliage provides shelter from the heat of a summer's day. Terra-cotta pots filled with plants and small trees complete the garden setting.

The wall of this Mediterranean-style garden in Saskatoon was made with hundreds of large stones gathered from the surrounding countryside. In summer it provides privacy and traps heat, lengthening the growing season; in winter it catches snow, which blankets the garden and protects many plants that might not survive otherwise.

GETTING *the* LOOK

❦ If you have a large garden, divide the space into smaller areas and separate at least one from the others with a wall, pergola, hedge of columnar juniper (a hardy substitute for the Mediterranean cypress) or a grove of trees. If your garden is small, enclose it almost entirely with one of the above, creating a private courtyard or patio.

❦ Use the appropriate construction materials. Old brick is suitable, and clay tiles fit the style perfectly although they may not be durable in cold areas here; consider using them on a roofed patio with an open fireplace for cool nights. Stucco is ideal for walls — a concrete and stucco wall is cheaper than a brick one; just remember to cap it with stone, or water will seep in.

❦ Cut back on lawn areas — instead, use terra cotta, colored gravel or concrete paving stones where you might have grass, or warm-toned pebbles set in concrete. Leave pockets for herbs such as thyme, or insert small colored tiles in a mosaic pattern. Set a birdbath or sundial in the center of a courtyard and surround it with sprawling plants.

✤ Color is important. Terra cotta, strong yellow, greens from verdigris to deep forest, and blues from turquoise to royal are classic Mediterranean colors. If you can't imagine using them for a garden wall or shed, use warm sand, ochre or terra cotta for major structures and add accents of hot color — mosaic tiles embedded in the wall or brightly painted plant pots, stair railings or tables and chairs. For an authentic look, try mortaring rows of broken crockery to large, straight-sided plant pots.

✤ Use appropriate garden furniture such as large canvas umbrellas, rough-hewn tables and café-style pieces.

✤ Water is an integral part of a Mediterranean garden, just as it was in Moorish and Persian gardens. Natural, woodsy ponds are seldom seen; formal and geometric is the norm. A square, raised pond, with its interior border inlaid with mosaic tiles or painted blue, would fit the style — as would a pond sunk in a stone terrace, with an arching stream of water as a fountain.

SELECTED PLANTS

✤ Cypress and olive trees are integral to the Mediterranean landscape, and although they aren't hardy here, substitutes can be made. Columnar juniper or even some varieties of cedar could stand in for cypress; the grey foliage and growing form of Russian olive evokes the tender olive tree.

✤ Most herbs are hardy here. Culinary and ornamental thymes, sage, tarragon, oregano and basil are commonly grown and remind the nose of Tuscany. In areas where lavender and rosemary are not hardy, they can be potted and wintered over indoors. Basil is grown from seed each spring.

✤ Grey-leaved plants like santolina are common in the hot Mediterranean climate. Appropriate additions here

With the sun glinting off the bright turquoise water of the formal swimming pool (above) and lush plantings in terra-cotta pots adding splashes of color, there's a definite feel of the Mediterranean in this sequestered urban garden.

include artemisias, lamb's-ears (*Stachys byzantina*) — and verbascum, a five-foot plant with small yellow flowers that also makes an architectural statement in the garden.

✤ Persian gardens were abundant with tulips, hyacinths and crocuses, all of which are hardy here.

✤ Yucca can take the place of spiky Mediterranean plants, and hardy sempervivums can substitute for tender low-growing succulents such as echeveria.

✤ For a true taste of the Mediterranean, grow lemon trees, oleander and jasmine in large containers and overwinter them indoors under lights.

SMALL URBAN SPACES

There are small gardens and then there are *small* gardens. An acre might seem cramped for some; others despair at squeezing themselves and their plants into a thousand square feet. And if the only space you have is the tiny backyard of an old Victorian house or the miniscule square in front of a row house — is a garden even possible? Confronting a big space may be daunting, but planning a garden in a space that leaves you underwhelmed can be, well — overwhelming.

WORKING *with a* SMALL SPACE

The secret to any successful garden design is planning, but a well-thought-out plan is especially important for gardeners with limited space. Mistakes can easily dominate a small garden.

Consider your space as another room of the house. What uses would you like to put it to? A place to entertain? A flower-filled sanctuary

The lush Vancouver garden (right) is a striking example of a successful design for a small urban space — with a deck for entertaining, high latticed fencing for privacy, a durable stone and gravel pathway, plus a square of cooling grass and masses of plants in pots, beds and on trellises.

Each of these gardens offers an attractive solution to the problem of limited space in a backyard. Planters overflowing with geraniums, licorice plant (Helichrysum petiolare) and heliotrope mark the step from the paved patio to the decking of a small back garden (above) in Vancouver. The weathered blue house (left), with its strong, clean lines and crisp white trim, is a natural focal point for this garden setting. A yard-wide pool (right) and abundant greenery offer tranquility in the middle of the city.

that invites relaxation at the end of the day? How do people enter and leave it? Would sliding doors onto a deck or terrace create a comfortable flow of traffic to the garden? If you plan to eat in the garden, where should the table and chairs go so they don't interfere with a door or gate?

❧ Your first priority is to establish privacy and mask unsightly views. In a city setting, it's unlikely you'll be able to "borrow" an attractive view — your garden may be bordered by boring walls or unsightly garages. Create a sense of enclosure with an attractive fence or hedge and look closer to home for a focal point.

❧ Find the area's best feature — a patch of dappled shade, the mellow texture of an old brick wall — then emphasize this focal point by designing your garden around it. Plan your design so that the eye is drawn to this area when viewing the garden. This can be done with paths, framing plants or structures.

❧ You can also establish a focal point by planting a specimen tree, mounting an attractive flower-filled urn on a plinth or leading the eye to a small, vine-covered arbor with a seat underneath.

❧ Attention to detail is also crucial — every inch of the garden design must be thought out carefully

so that everything relates in a pleasing way.

❧ Although you'll be gardening in a small space, consider ongoing maintenance when finalizing your plans. Because every detail is close and within view, it's important to keep the garden tidy. The upside is that small gardens, by virtue of their size, are easy to keep under control — without the edging, weeding and lawn-mowing that large gardens require.

❧ Since small urban gardens receive a lot of concentrated foot traffic, consider replacing a lawn with generous paths and patios, ground covers and other foliage plants.

CREATING *the* ILLUSION *of* SPACE

❧ Small city lots are often long and narrow. Divide the garden crosswise into different areas of interest to direct the focus away from the narrow length. You could design a sitting area near the house, with an assortment of container plants as accents; a simple pond, surrounded by ornamental grasses and hostas; and a secluded spot near the back of the garden, framed by an ivy-covered arbor or arch. A path might weave from area to area, drawing the visitor onward and creating a sense of discovery in a small place.

❧ Use a variety of paving materials, such as gravel, stones and brick, and a change of direction in paths to help divide up the space — much as runners and rugs do in a house.

❧ When installing a deck or patio, try to position a section of it down a step or two — or create a slight change in grade in another area of the garden. A multi-level landscape fools the eye into thinking that it's seeing a larger space because it has to travel a greater distance while taking everything in. A turn in a path also makes a walk through a garden seem longer.

❧ Vertical spaces can be used to create a sense of spaciousness. Although living boundaries like yew or privet are soft and subtle, they take time to mature — and also claim valuable space. Walls, fences and trellises provide visual interest the minute you put them up.

❧ Be creative and decorate fences with old pieces of wrought iron or pretty terra-cotta ornaments, or put candles in sconces to light the garden at night. Fill wall baskets with trailing plants, or soften and blur perimeter fences with climbing plants such as morning glories or English ivy. An espaliered fruit tree or climbing rose makes a striking specimen on a section of a wall or fence.

❧ If the entrance from the house to the garden is considerably above grade, use the stairs down to the garden to hold pots of flowers — or build steeply racked planters beside the stairs for a big hit of color.

SELECTED PLANTS

Choosing plants for a small garden requires careful thought, and the overall size of each specimen is just one of the considerations.

❧ Close attention should be paid to the mature size of trees and shrubs you add to the landscape. Small-leaved trees, such as mountain ash, are more appropriate than bulky maples and oaks. Limb-up trees to allow sunlight to filter into the garden and permit seating or planting space underneath.

❧ The standard tree form of some popular shrubs is a good choice and suits the scale of most small gardens. These have been grafted onto the top of a single stem or trunk. The stem stays about 5 feet (150 cm) high but the grafted-on branches grow full and dense. Popular standards include Walker weeping peashrub (*Caragana arborescens* 'Walker'), weeping mulberry (*Morus alba* 'Pendula'), wintercreeper (*Euonymus fortunei* cultivars) and purple-leaved sand cherry (*Prunus* X *cistena*).

❧ Whatever trees or shrubs you choose, be prepared to prune them regularly to keep everything within bounds and maintain your overall design.

❧ Thre is no room in small gardens for plants that don't hold your interest for more than a few weeks. Look for perennials with foliage that's attractive even when the plant is not in bloom; flowering shrubs with interesting branch patterns and texture, even in winter; and trees with autumn tints and colorful bark in winter.

❧ For clothing walls, arbors, trellises and pergolas, plant

With space at a premium, the owner of a postage-stamp townhouse garden (left) used every available inch of space to fill his urban oasis with plants — in hanging baskets and wooden planters, in terra-cotta pots on the stairs and around the deck, in tiny beds, and even climbing up the wooden fence.

climbers. Annual vines include cup-and-saucer vine (*Cobaea scandens*), morning glory (*Ipomea* spp.), canary creeper (*Trapaeolum peregrinum*) and scarlet runner beans. Perennials vines like wisteria and climbing hydrangea (*H. anomala petiolaris*) generally take longer to cover a fence or trellis than annuals, but grow vigorously once established. For faster-growing perennials, try honeysuckle (*Lonicera* spp.) or silver-lace vine (*Polygonum aubertii*). Clematis offers many different species to suit varied garden conditions. Climbing roses work well, too.

❧ Limit the number of plants, but make lavish use of the ones you choose. Shades of green or soft pastels with lots of white are more restful than bright colors, scattered throughout the garden, that fight for attention and give the eye no place to rest.

❧ Use restraint when placing eye-catching plants — too many variegated, large-leaved or gold foliage plants can overwhelm a small garden, and create a busy impression that lacks unity.

❧ Avoid plants that self-seed in pavement or brick, plants with far-ranging suckers or trees with shallow roots that may displace paths or patios.

❧ Don't use too many plants with an upright form; they'll lead the eye out of the design — and the garden. Instead, concentrate on plants with weeping, rounded or horizontal forms that center the eye on the design.

ENHANCING *your* SPACE

There are various ways to make a small space seem bigger and to add visual interest.

❧ A window cut into a fence, perhaps to take advantage of a view, creates a feeling of greater space in the garden. A *trompe l'oeil* scene on a wall has the same effect, and so

can a mirror. Using a mirror behind a statue bordered by greenery, for example, creates the impression that the mirrored area is actually another verdant room. Place mirrors with care, however, to avoid reflecting an unattractive element in the garden.

❧ To blur the distinction between indoors and out, place house plants around the entrance from the house to the

garden, and install large sliding doors so that the room flows into the garden. Carry the decoration of the interior into the garden by matching color schemes and furniture styles.

❧ When choosing structures for your small garden, make sure they blend with the scale and style of your house. Summerhouses and gazebos can overwhelm a small property; instead, work an angled pergola or wide arbor into your design to allow for seating in a shady corner.

❧ Container plants and hanging baskets are a good way to fill a small space with the maximum amount of greenery.

❧ Thin, dark, wrought-iron furniture is more appropriate than heavy wooden chairs and tables. Tables with glass tops are pleasing and unobtrusive.

❧ Wrought-iron gates create a barrier but still permit an enticing view of the garden within.

❧ In a small space, tiny details are more pleasing than large or overbearing elements. Unusual bits of driftwood, a collection of pebbles at the turn of a path or a small found object half-hidden by hosta leaves creates an interesting vignette without overwhelming the design.

❧ Even the smallest garden has room for the soothing sound of water. A lion's-head fountain, mounted on a brick pillar, or a small bubbler that just breaks the surface in a broad terra-cotta pot takes up little space.

❧ Use fragrance to add another dimension to the garden. Scatter seed for night-scented stock (*Matthiola longipetala*) — an unobtrusive lavender-colored annual that perfumes the evening air — throughout a border, or grow fragrant lilies in a pot near a bench.

❧ To get the most use out of your small garden, install outdoor lighting. This lets you enjoy evenings in the garden in warm weather, and allows quiet enjoyment of the winterscape from inside the house.

Gardening with style high above the city streets is a challenge — especially when space is limited. The inventive owner of the rooftop garden (left) divided the area into smaller living spaces, perfect for reading or entertaining. Unpainted wood throughout, and the casual white metal table and chair, give the space a sunny and relaxed feel.

THE GARDEN *in* WINTER

For many Canadians, the garden is out of mind the minute icy blasts blow. But just because plants are blanketed with snow, the garden isn't gone — it's simply stripped back to its bare bones. A properly designed garden should be beautiful in every season, even winter — not as riotously, colorfully alive as it is in summer, perhaps, but beautiful nonetheless.

Too often, however, our winter gardens are charmless repositories of exposed garbage cans, commercial composters or central air-conditioning units. As soon as frost kills the foliage, these elements become the unsightly centerpieces of the garden, and greet us every morning until spring.

Winter reveals the importance of a good garden plan. The framework is provided by structural elements such as paths, fences, arbors and trellises, as well as by the proper placement of evergreens and deciduous shrubs and trees. These are permanent features in the garden, part of the backdrop in the summer but much more visible in winter.

❧ Arbors and trellises that support roses or vines in summer stand as design elements on their own in winter, adding interest by casting shadows on the snow.

❧ A flagstone path that takes second place to the beds of perennials it winds through in summer looks wonderful in late March glistening with melting ice.

❧ Iron gates, birdbaths and statuary — bare or covered with snow — take on new character as focal points in the garden.

❧ Evergreen hedges, trellis screens, and walls of brick or stucco hide composters or garbage cans more effectively than deciduous plants, as well as adding interesting shape and structure to the winter scene.

The success, or failure, of a garden design is most evident in winter, when the garden is stripped to its bare bones — the paths, fences, water details and plantings that shape the landscape.

❧ Create a winter arrangement visible from the living-room window — for example, move a bench into view at the end of the garden and flank it with an empty weatherproof pot filled with branches.

❧ Color warms up a winter garden and gives it personality. Create a *trompe l'oeil* scene on the side of the garden shed, or simply wash it with terra cotta or mustard paint. Paint the finials of a fence mauve or bright blue, or an Adirondack chair bright yellow.

❧ Simple features like a low, clipped box hedge outlining a path capture the eye in winter; the subtle colors and strong shape of a chunk of granite in a bed of low-growing cotoneaster also come into their own in the softer light of the season.

NATURE'S *own* DESIGN ELEMENTS

Certain plants work well in a garden year-round. Conifers and evergreens are obvious examples, but are often chosen without much thought — and without making the most of their varied colors. Observe them in the depth of winter, and you soon realize their tones vary from a deep purple-tinged green to dull gold and bronze.

❧ Pines, hemlocks and yews stay a fresh green until spring; spruce changes to shades of blue; wintercreeper (*Euonymus fortunei*), a broadleaf evergreen, turns a dull bronzy-green in cold weather and mature plants carry orange berries encased in beige husks.

❧ Rhododendrons remain dark green until spring, and their drooping leaves add texture to a bed of shrubs.

❧ The branches of deciduous trees and shrubs display their distinctive personalities in winter — some like crooked fingers, others straight or arching — and they take on a magical air when dusted with snow or coated with clear ice after a freezing rain.

❧ Even borderline ornamental shrubs, looking like small monks wandering the garden, assume character when swathed in the burlap that helps them survive the winter.

Pleasing Shapes

❧ Untrimmed white cedar hedges have a shaggy look that works well in winter.

❧ Tall conifers have majestic presence and offer wind and weather protection on the periphery of a garden.

❧ Low mugo pines look like cushions, especially when topped with fresh snow.

A WINTER GARDEN *for* BIRDS

❧ A bird feeder adds color and variety to a winter garden, attracting flashy jays and cardinals that enliven the grey landscape. Seed scattered on the ground brings small sparrows and juncos, lively birds that make up in activity for their relatively plain apparel.

❧ Plant shrubs close to the feeder so birds have a place to perch —

and don't forget about water. To keep water in a pond from freezing, use a small heater (also good for birdbaths) or keep water moving with a recirculating pump near the surface.

❧ Grow plants that provide berries through the winter — including highbush cranberry (*Viburnum trilobum*), firethorn, hollies and roses that produce hips.

*Ornamental grasses make a striking statement
in the winter garden — with red-osier dogwood (above) and
with sedum 'Autumn Joy' (right).*

❧ Topiary shapes, from straight or curved clipped hedges to spirals and balls, add formal structure to the landscape.

Effective Contrasts
Evergreens and conifers need to be offset by the stark shapes and the various bark textures and colors of deciduous trees and shrubs. There are limitless choices.
❧ Burning bush (*Euonymus alata*) is fiery red until its leaves fall, then reveals branches with winged, corky bark tinged with green.
❧ Cherry trees have bark speckled like a starling's breast.

❧ Mature beech trees have bark that looks like a gnarled grey hide.
❧ A tatarian dogwood that's been kept well trimmed to allow new growth to dominate has bark a cinnamon or bright red color.

Other Plants That Contribute Winter Interest
❧ The red fruit of mountain ash, highbush cranberry and rockspray; the colorful hips of rugosa rose (a favorite food of birds); the mauve berries of beautybush (*Callicarpa japonica*); and the soft moth-brown keys of amur maple.

Hydrangea in winter is as pretty as it is in summer. Its lovely snowball-shaped blooms, now dried to a dusty cream color, make an impressive dried-flower arrangement — or can be tied at the stem with ribbon and hung as ornaments on the Christmas tree.

❧ Ornamental cabbage and kale, in color combinations of cream, green, carmine and rose, provide color that lasts until hard frost.

❧ Ornamental grasses in tones from beige to gold; the brown or black seedheads of perennials, such as purple coneflower (*Echinacea purpurea*) or black-eyed Susan (*Rudbeckia hirta*) in brown and black, peeking above the snow.

SELECTED PLANTS

❧ WEEPING RED JADE CRAB APPLE (*Malus* 'Red Jade') and SARGENT'S CRAB APPLE (*M. sargentii*) are striking in the winter landscape, and birds enjoy the red fruit.

❧ CHERRY TREES have bark and branches that give them winter interest.

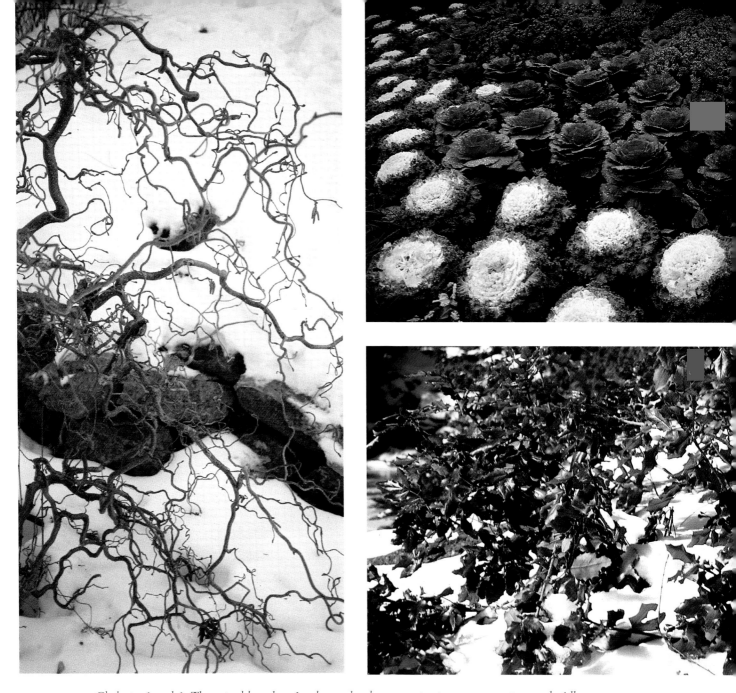

Clockwise from left: The twisted branches of corkscrew hazel create an intricate pattern against newly fallen snow; a colorful autumn border of ornamental kale; Oregon holly (Mahonia aquifolium).

🌾 CORKSCREW HAZEL (*Corylus avellana* 'Contorta') has twisted branches that are eye-catching in winter.

🌾 WINTERCREEPER (*Euonymus fortunei* 'Goldspot' or 'Emerald Gaiety') has attractive variegated leaves and makes a good ground cover or vine.

🌾 SIBERIAN DOGWOOD (*Cornus alba* 'Sibirica'), with its deep-red branches, makes a striking contrast in the winter garden.

🌾 BALTIC IVY (*Hedera helix* 'Baltica') has typical three-cornered leaves and stays deep green in winter.

🌾 MOUNTAIN ASH (*Sorbus aucuparia*) has red fruit birds like.

🌾 'BLUE PRINCE' and 'BLUE PRINCESS' HOLLY (*Ilex* X *meserveae*) have shiny, leathery thorned leaves, but you must plant both to get berries.

🌾 SMALLER PLANTS — ornamental grasses and perennials, such as astilbe, sedum and yarrow, look good both bare and topped with snow. Yucca maintains its broad, spiked leaves year-round. Plant some winter aconite (*Eranthis hyemalis*), for bright yellow blooms that peek through the March snow.

CHAPTER THREE

WATER
in the
GARDEN

*W*hether it's the refreshing
splash of an ornate fountain or the soothing stillness
of a lily-filled pond, water adds its own magic
to any garden. It becomes a focal point —
a shimmering oasis to which we happily retreat,
often for hours at a time.

Water is a welcome feature in any garden. In a formal garden, a rectangular reflecting pool complements the clipped hedges and structured beds. A raised, mosaic tile-lined pool with an arching spray of water works well in a Mediterranean garden where it evokes memories of the Moors, who used water in their gardens wherever possible. A pond surrounded with informal plantings and areas of river stones, covered with lily pads and filled with darting fish, completes a country garden.

Whatever its style, a pond is a focal point — and, happily, no longer the exclusive property of the rich. With today's choice of liners and recirculating pumps, anyone can add a water feature to a garden. But before you put shovel to earth, think about the type of pond you'd like and where you'd like to put it, then spend some time researching the different styles and the cost of materials.

The LOCATION of a POND

❧ A pond should be far enough from big trees so that roots don't pose problems, and leaves — which use up oxygen as they decompose and upset the pond's balance — don't fall into it.

There are countless ways to create a water feature in a garden — from a large natural-looking pond (left) to a simple hollowed-out stone (top), with its single floating bloom.

⚜ Choose a level site, or one on a very slight slope, to avoid construction complications. Make sure the site is accessible if you need to use heavy equipment.

⚜ To support flowering plants, your pond needs to be in sun. Waterlilies, which add to the beauty of a pond, need six or seven hours of sunlight a day; their large green pads shade the water, protecting fish and helping control the growth of algae, which thrive in sunlight.

⚜ Ponds near the house make electrical hook-up of circulating pumps and lighting simpler. They can also be enjoyed from indoors and become a focal point when viewed from a living-room or dining-room window. But don't put one so close to the house that you disturb the foundation or interfere with buried cables when digging.

⚜ On the other hand, a pond hidden in the corner of the yard is a delightful oasis and, if it contains a fountain or is fed by a small waterfall hooked up to a recirculating pump, its sound can be an invitation to visit.

⚜ Avoid windy sites — plants won't thrive, pond water will evaporate rapidly, fountains will spray outside the pool and no one will want to sit there.

PLAY *it* SAFE *with* WATER

⚜ Pools are not a good idea if you have young children who play, unsupervised, in the garden; they can drown in even a few inches of water.

⚜ Some municipalities limit the depth of unfenced pools and may require a building permit. Check the by-laws before you start digging.

⚜ The edges of any pool or pond should be solid and firm to prevent anyone from slipping into the water.

⚜ Water and electricity are a dangerous combination. Unless you are experienced, have any electrical work done by a professional.

POND STYLES

Once you've selected a location for your pond, think about its style — which will also be dictated by the style of the garden. An obviously man-made pool in a formal style is far easier to build than an informal pool and waterfall intended to look like part of the landscape. There is nothing less appealing in a garden than a failed attempt at a natural pond — one with over-defined curves, a stiff border of stones and no connection to its surroundings.

⚜ If your garden is flat with geometrically arranged borders and pathways, a simple formal pond with raised sides and a small fountain is perfectly appropriate. Alternatively, the pond could be sunk almost level with the ground and surrounded with a broad border of flagstone. A raised or sunken pond can be a stunning focal point in a structured garden, set at the end of a straight path with a handsome bench beside it. The tableau could be enclosed with a hedge and planted from pond to perimeter with low herbs, turning it into a fragrant hideaway.

⚜ Square or round ponds also look good in a deck or patio, either flush with the surface or with raised sides of

The shape and style of a pond or pool should reflect its surroundings. An informal pond (above), with its natural edging of rocks, suits the casual style of a country garden. The clean lines of a classic rectangular pool (left) are appropriate for a more formal garden.

wood or stone. A pond in a deck built several feet above ground level will have to be fully boxed and supported by beams under the deck; a pond in a deck raised a few inches to a foot or so above ground should be encased to ground level in a wood frame before digging to the correct depth and installing the liner.

❧ Informal ponds with curved shapes and natural edgings, such as fieldstone and rocks, are perfect partners for gardens with winding paths of gravel or bark chips and loose cottage-style plantings. Simple shapes are more effective than serpentine curves — before you outline the pond (a garden hose or a rope helps you try various shapes), observe nature's ponds, which gravitate to low-lying areas and follow the shape of the terrain.

❧ Natural ponds also fit easily into rock gardens. A small

pond, perhaps a preformed fiberglass shape embedded in the soil and edged with creeping plants and stone, could sustain a fish or two and a water hyacinth. If the rock garden is graded down a hill, two such ponds (the upper one smaller than the lower) could be joined by a small cascade of water.

❧ A yard with a change of grade lends itself naturally to a waterfall, but you can make one in a flat space if you keep the waterfall low and place it near a fence or a corner of the garden, where the water can be made to look like it is flowing into the garden from another source. Bank the earth excavated for the pond on one side to create the waterfall.

❧ Natural ponds don't necessarily need a waterfall to provide the soothing sound of water. Small ripples that break the surface or spill over stones are also charming. A submersible pump buried under stones at the bottom of the water can be regulated to give surface ripples or a bubble of water. Alternatively, the pump can be used to recirculate the water in a waterfall or fountain.

❧ The mood of a northern cottage can be evoked with a stone-filled, boulder-edged pond that begins under your deck and has gentle ripples of water flowing over the stones. To complete the look, plant low ground covers and moss to creep over the groups of boulders at the far end of the pond, and back them with dwarf evergreens and small deciduous trees pruned to look like a mature, windswept forest. Think of the skyline across a northern lake and you'll have the idea.

❧ Still ponds have a peaceful appeal, but since they won't be heard, it's important to place them where they can be seen. They're effective sunk into a deck or patio adjoining the French doors. Classic urns and old cooking pots make good small reflecting ponds. Be sure to include oxygenating water plants like pond weed and hornwort to maintain the natural balance of the water. A waterlily or water hyacinth adds the finishing touch.

LINERS

Expert pond installers agree that flexible liners are the best option for backyard ponds. Large natural ponds on country properties don't usually have to be lined since they have a clay bottom — but it's best to consult a soil expert or engineer first. Concrete, once the only option for ornamental ponds, is sturdy and long-lasting but difficult to work with; it can also crack after a few years if it's not poured properly, and the lime in it is toxic to fish unless a sealer is applied. Although initially cheaper than flexible liners, concrete winds up being more expensive if you add the cost of sealing and repairing cracks.

❧ Preformed liners of moulded plastic or fiberglass come in limited shapes and sizes, and some are too shallow to support fish and water plants. A depth of 24 inches (60 cm) is fine for waterlilies, but fish and frogs need a section of water that extends below the

THINK SMALL — TINY PONDS *are a* CLASS ACT

Even a tiny porch or balcony, or a small corner of the yard, can be enlivened with a water feature. Here are a few ideas to whet your imagination.

STILL WATER

Plunk a pygmy waterlily, a few marginal or surface plants and half a dozen goldfish into a container lined (if necessary) with a nontoxic, waterproof material and fill with water. Some container suggestions:

❧ A wood or stone trough or wooden box.
❧ A half-barrel (kits are often available from water garden suppliers and garden centers).
❧ An old porcelain or earthenware sink or tub.

MOVING WATER

The soothing sounds of water are easily available — all you need is a submersible pump to recirculate the water through a small fountain, jet or spout, and a container for the water.

Some suggestions:
❧ A pebble fountain, made by immersing a small pump in a half-barrel or buried moulded pond filled to the surface with water and pebbles or cobbles.
❧ A Japanese ping fountain — water falls from a spout in single drops through a series of tiny pools hollowed into stones set like steps in a wall or a slope.

❧ A hollowed-out bamboo pole, set in a bamboo frame, that recirculates water into a basin.
❧ A wall-mounted spout that recirculates water from the pump in a pond or basin below. These come in a wide range of styles, from lavabo units to gargoyle-like faces. Hide the hose carrying the water behind the fence or wall, or insert it into a pipe or decorative tubing and disguise with ivy.

Moulded ponds come in many shapes, cost more than other pond liners and are trickier to install, but they're easier to repair if pierced. The form should sit on a level base, with the rim slightly above grade. Backfill firmly.

Above-ground ponds are good solutions when excavating is difficult, and they bring plants and fish closer to the eye. A flexible liner or moulded pond form can be used, but sides need to be well supported with bricks, railway ties or poured concrete.

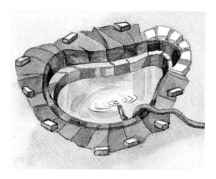

With a flexible liner, you can create any design and the pond can be as deep as you like. Once the hole is dug, use newspaper or commercial underlay to protect liner. Fit liner into place and partly fill with water to tighten.

frost line if they are to overwinter in the pond. Getting a moulded liner perfectly level can be tricky, and disguising its rigid edges with plants is sometimes more difficult than with flexible liners. On the plus side, it requires a shallower excavation and is easier to repair.

❧ Flexible liners allow the pond-builder more scope in shape and depth, and they're available in a variety of sizes, thicknesses and price ranges; be sure to choose one that's resistant to ultraviolet light. Don't use a swimming-pool liner — the chemicals it's treated with to deter algae growth are toxic to fish.

❧ Butyl is probably the most expensive liner (close to $2 a square foot), but it comes with a 20-year warranty and has been known to last 50 years. EPDM, another rubber liner, is a low-talc version of a roofing product and less expensive than butyl, about $1.50 a foot. Both resist cracking at low temperatures and are easy to work with. Don't use the cheaper, roofing EPDM — the talc in it will harm pond life.

❧ PVC (polyvinyl chloride) compares in price to EPDM and is sold in various grades. The newest PVC liners are UV-stabilized and frost-resistant, and last 10 to 20 years.

❧ Experts advise against using a polyethylene liner. Although much less expensive, polyethylene tears easily and degrades quickly, and may need to be replaced in 3 or 4 years.

❧ Ask the shop owner's advice when choosing the type and thickness of liner; thickness varies from 15 mil to over 40 mil. Thinner liners are more flexible, but may be susceptible to the sharp claws of visiting pets or raccoons, or to rocks falling off the edging.

MAKING *the* POND

Once you've laid out the pond's shape, the next step is the excavation. You'll want to plan for a shelf approximately 8 inches (20 cm) below the surface and wide enough to hold pots of perimeter plants. A deep area in the middle or at one end is necessary to overwinter fish and pond plants. This should be below the frost line, probably 3 or 4 feet (90 to 120 cm), but consult a local contractor for the correct depth.

To calculate the amount of flexible liner required, add 2 feet (60 cm), plus twice the depth, to both the length and the width of the pond; a simpler method is to take the pond's dimensions to the shop and have them do it for you. Liners must extend several inches from the pond's edges.

STEP I

❧ Dig out the area with a shovel or a backhoe down as far as the shelf, sloping the sides an inch (2.5 cm) for every 3 inches (7.5 cm) of drop. Make a gentler slope for crumbly or sandy soil. Leave 8 to 10 inches (20 to 25 cm) of width for the shelf, and dig out the center of the pond. Remember that most waterlilies need about 2 feet (60 cm) of water. A deeper well in the bottom to overwinter fish should take up roughly 30 percent of the pond's area. Level the earth of the upper shelf. Make sure the edges of the pond itself are level by laying a spirit level on a straight plank across the pond.

The secret to creating a successful pond is to make it look like part of the landscape — a work of nature, not of man.

STEP 2

❦ Remove stones and sharp roots from the excavation, then put down a layer of wet sand. Over this, lay landscape fabric (also called geotextile), carpet scraps or a thick layer of newspapers. Now you're ready to fit the excavation with the liner.

STEP 3

❦ Place the folded liner in the middle of the excavation and unfold into position without stretching. Let it sit this way in the sun for a while to soften. Anchor edges with smooth stones. When the liner seems malleable, smooth the bottom level first, pleating in the wrinkles carefully as you work. Once you've finished the lowest level, fill it with water to hold the liner in place.

STEP 4

❦ Smooth the upper shelf area from the edge of the pond — or stand in the center in rubber boots or hip waders, making sure no stones that could pierce the liner are embedded in the soles.

STEP 5

❦ Fill the pool to within an inch of the top, releasing the stones holding the liner in place as it tightens.

To install a preformed pond liner, dig down to its depth and slightly wider all around. Use a level to ensure position, and backfill firmly around the shelves and outer edge, leaving the edge slightly above the surface.

EDGING

The edging is crucial, since it should tie the pond to the garden as naturally as possible and hide all evidence of liners and other construction materials. Achieving the right look for a formal pond is much easier than trying to disguise the traces of an informal man-made pond.

❧ Large, flat flagstones, laid on a bed of sand and extending a maximum of 2 inches (5 cm) over the edge, make a relatively simple edging that looks natural.

❧ A raised square pond could be edged with wide rock slabs that provide a place to sit.

❧ Bricks in a radial pattern look good around a circular ground-level pond, but be sure they're flush with the surrounding grass or soil. Leave a long overlap on the flexible liner and bring it up under and behind the bricks. It's advisable to mortar the bricks in place.

❧ A few rocks placed on the underwater shelf and breaking the surface of the water add to the informal look of a natural pond. Place a pad of landscape fabric under them to avoid the risk of damaging a flexible liner.

❧ Don't outline an informal pond with a regimented row of flat stones or rocks. Place rocks of several sizes in groups, near the edge, as you'd see them in nature. Combine flat rocks and smaller pebbles, and allow small plants, such as creeping ground covers or low grasses, to grow as they might at the water's edge. Many of the larger stones might have to be cemented in place for stability.

❧ Pebble beaches are perfect for natural ponds. When laying the flexible liner, make a wide, shallow shelf at one end of the pond with a curb on its inside edge, near the surface of the water. Use bricks or round-edge pavers for the curb and cover with newspaper or geotextile before fitting the liner over the top. Behind the curb, the liner should drop a few inches and gradually slope up to the level of the rest of the garden. Cover the hollow behind the curb with small pebbles.

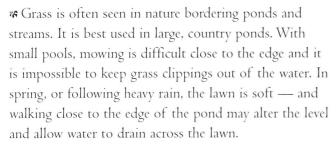

Once a water feature has been constructed, add the finishing touches that make it uniquely yours — a whimsical statue, stone sculptures or a delightful carved fish that spouts water.

❧ Grass is often seen in nature bordering ponds and streams. It is best used in large, country ponds. With small pools, mowing is difficult close to the edge and it is impossible to keep grass clippings out of the water. In spring, or following heavy rain, the lawn is soft — and walking close to the edge of the pond may alter the level and allow water to drain across the lawn.

❧ Boggy areas, rich with plants that love damp conditions, are also seen beside ponds in nature. A boggy area can be made the same way as a pebble beach — just make the shelf deeper and fill with soil instead of pebbles.

PLANTS

Aquatic plants divide into three categories — surface plants, with leaves at or just above the water surface; marginal plants, growing in shallow water but with leaves and flowers well above the surface; and the oxygenators, which grow underwater.

Surface Plants

❧ Waterlilies (*Nymphea*) and lotuses (*Nelumbo*) grow in pots underwater, but they have broad floating leaves and beautiful flowers; waterlilies need calm water and won't grow well in small pools with a waterfall or fountain. Their pads provide excellent hiding spots for fish and protect them from the hot sun.

❧ Fairy moss (*Azolla caroliniana*), water hyacinth (*Eichornia crassipes*) and water lettuce (*Pistia stratioides*) are free-floating plants that move about the pool's surface at the whim of the wind, with their roots trailing in the water. They may become invasive in a small pool, but are easy to remove.

❧ As a rule, plants with floating foliage should cover up to two-thirds of the pond's surface.

Marginal Plants

❧ Many marginal plants have showy flowers. They extend the season of bloom, and the different leaf shapes add to the texture of the pond planting. Some worth considering are marsh marigold (*Caltha palustris*), a yellow spring bloomer; Japanese iris (*Iris ensata*), in a wide range of pastel shades, early summer; flowering rush (*Butomus umbellatus*), pink, late summer; and dwarf cattail (*Typha minima*), with grass-like foliage and brown seedheads in fall.

Oxygenators

❧ The hard-working oxygenators are fully submerged and, as their name implies, produce oxygen. They're planted in pots placed at the bottom of the pond, and their graceful foliage weaves up through the water, cleansing it of toxins and squeezing out algae by competing for nutrients.

❧ Canada pond weed (*Elodea*), arrowhead (*Sagittaria*) and ribbon grass (*Vallisnaria*) — also called tape grass or eel grass — are common oxygenators. Allow one bunch for every 2 to 3 square feet (.18 to .27 sq m) of pond surface.

ALGAE

This is an unwelcome pond plant. Direct sunlight, the very condition one wants for a pond, can cause algae to "bloom" and turn the water a bright, murky green. The best way to fight algae is not with chemicals but with other plants. As noted earlier, lily and lotus leaves block out some of the light algae thrive on, and floating plants (as well as oxygenators, and marginal plants to a lesser degree) compete for the organic material algae need. Water snails and tadpoles gobble up algae and other organic debris. You can also prevent algae flare-up by not overfeeding fish and by keeping their numbers under control.

FISH

Fish round out a pond. Their presence means a complete little ecosystem is in operation. Goldfish and Japanese koi, both of which are a species of carp, are the most common ones used, but others like shubunkin, as well as fancy goldfish like calico fantails and lionheads, are available. Be forewarned — koi need a large pond to grow in.

When considering the number of fish you should buy for your pond, there are two important rules to follow.

❧ There should not be more than 1 inch (2.5 cm) of fish per square foot (.09 sq m) of surface, or per 100 gallons (450 L) of water.

❧ Start with fewer. Fish grow fast and sometimes they procreate, or enter the pond as eggs attached to the pond plants you buy.

Wait a couple of weeks after you've put plants in and any algae bloom has died down before introducing fish in your pond. Put them in the pond in the plastic bags of water in which you bought them and leave the bag in place for about an hour. Add a bit of pond water to the bag and leave it for another 10 or 15 minutes. If the sun is strong, place a small towel over the bag to shade it. Then gently open the bag and let the fish swim out.

In a well-balanced pond, fish don't need a lot of supplementary food. In summer, feed them three or four times a week and only as much as they'll eat in 5 minutes.

Overwintering Fish

Preparing fish for winter is important. Fish in ponds less than 24 inches (60 cm) deep should be brought indoors for winter and held in aquariums. But even in cold parts of the country, fish can be overwintered in ponds that extend below the frost line (a good argument for digging the pond deep enough in the first place).

❧ Make sure the pond is clear of fall leaves, which will break down and add ammonia and other toxins to the water, possibly killing the fish. Stop feeding fish as soon as the water temperature drops to 10°C (50°F) — their systems are starting to slow down for winter hibernation and they won't digest the food.

❧ The pond's surface should have an ice-free area at least once a week to let toxic gases escape. There are several ways to do this: You can leave the recirculating pump operating near the surface of the water, not at the bottom, where it will churn up the warmer water and harm the fish. You can let the pond freeze over, then melt a small area on top (never chop the hole — the shock waves could kill the fish) and pump out some of the water, leaving an air space. Or you could half-drain the pond and cover it with boards, leaving an air space, and top it with bales of straw for insulation. Floating de-icers and submersible, thermostatically controlled heaters are also available. An inexpensive bubbler will also keep the pond from freezing.

CHAPTER FOUR

COLOR
in the
GARDEN

*T*here's more to
color in the garden than just a pleasing color
scheme. Some colors work optical magic, making
a tiny space seem bigger, while others brighten
our spirits with a burst of clear blue or
sunny yellow. Even the muted tones of green
or grey foliage have an impact on the overall
design. Here's how to make the most of color
in your own garden.

THE PRINCIPLES
of COLOR

Whatever your personal taste, there's a larger rationale at work when it comes to designing a pleasing color scheme for your garden. You need a basic understanding of how color works in order to use it effectively. Some colors trick the eye, bringing distant vistas closer or making a tiny space seem bigger. Colors also create mood — lush green ferns in a tranquil woodland garden are a good example — or enhance structures such as fences or arbors.

Red is the longest wavelength visible to the human eye, while violet is the shortest. In between are the colors of the rainbow — orange, yellow, green, blue and indigo. This is a fundamental principle that should be remembered when it comes to garden design — red flowers appear closer than they are, while blue and violet recede into the distance. In other words, to make an area appear smaller or to draw attention to a distant piece of sculpture, plant some red-blossom or red-foliage plants at the outer boundary of the garden or near the sculpture. To visually enlarge a small garden or create a lengthening vista, use blue, mauve or violet.

It has been shown that the lens of the eye is in natural focus when looking at green; to see red, a refocus of the lens is required and a further refocus must occur to see blue and violet. By using sufficient green foliage, the garden designer helps the eye make a smooth focal transition between these or any other strong contrasting colors. White is also recommended to reconcile harshly contrasting colors in the garden, but it works better joining pale colors rather than bright ones, where it actually accentuates the contrast. Greens and greys or hazy white plants such as baby's-breath and artemisia are more effective in linking difficult colors. White, of course, is essential in designing a garden for nighttime enjoyment.

Some gardeners love the jolt of vivid scarlets with golden yellows, while others find this visually exhausting and prefer gentle shades of pink, mauve and purple, or an all-foliage scheme of soothing greens.

Selecting *a* Color Scheme

S ome gardens are a jumble of color. Tawny orange daylilies nuzzle up to hot-pink roses, magenta phlox elbow mustard-yellow yarrow, and scarlet poppies consort with pale pink peonies. Disordered profusion like this is what English cottage gardens are all about, and no one disputes their inimitable charm — although it takes a sure hand to mix such strong colors without jarring the eye. Green or grey foliage or hazy white plants are often used to buffer the vibrancy in this type of garden.

❧ There are many reasons for selecting a color scheme for your garden, and the most obvious is

personal choice. Today's popular trend is pink — from the palest flesh through mauve and rose to deep carmine. If you love pink, your choice of plant material is unlimited. And pink has proven therapeutic value; psychologists in correctional institutions have long been aware that pink-walled rooms lessen aggressive behavior.

❧ Garden color schemes are also chosen to complement indoor decor. If the walls of your living room are pale lemon, the flower arranger in you might choose a garden palette of mauves, blues and light yellows. Or you may enjoy the crispness of blue and white at your dinner table, so you grow veronica and delphinium, shasta daisies and baby's-breath.

❧ But most gardens are planned for total effect — to complement both the interior and exterior of the home. When planning your garden, pause to view it from the places it's most apt to be seen, perhaps a deck, patio or window. Consider the mood and color scheme of the room you're standing in as well as the fence or shrubs in the background; they're important components of the scene. For example, your neighbor's deep brown fence will influence the plant colors you choose — you might gravitate to a sunset range of golden yellows, copper oranges and burnished reds, colors that glow against a dark background.

❧ Your front garden is likely to be seen mainly from the street, so the color of your home or the

foundation plantings are the most important influences. If, for example, your house is an orange-tone brick, don't choose flowers or shrubs in the lilac or magenta range, such as the otherwise beautiful and hardy rhododendron 'P.J.M.' It will look ghastly against the clashing orange brick wall.

Gertrude Jekyll, the turn-of-the-century grand dame of English garden design, created grand perennial borders in response to the Victorian style of growing vast plots of annuals in garish combinations. She had a great deal to say about her

The color of architectural elements — such as a fence, the exterior of a house, a brick wall or a neighbor's shed — influences our choice of plants for the garden. Flowers in complementary or contrasting hues are preferable to ones that clash with the surroundings.

contemporaries who were, in her view, misusing color. "They have no idea," she complained, "of using precious jewels in a setting of quiet environment, or of suiting the color of flowering groups to that of the neighboring foliage, thereby enhancing the value of both, or of massing related or harmonious colorings so as to lead up to their most powerful and brilliant effects."

With Jekyll's admonition as a guide, let's begin with a look at the hot spectrum — the golden yellows, oranges and reds, sometimes called the sunset colors.

Bright-orange Marigolds (Tagetes) *and Dahlias* ▲

Asiatic Hybrid Lily (Lilium) ▲

COLOR
IN THE GARDEN

HOT GARDENS

Hot gardens are for the adventurous, not the faint of heart. Warm, spectral hues jump at the eye, creating either a pleasant jolt or a nasty jar, depending on their placement. A large garden can accommodate a sweeping border of hot colors, but owners of tiny spaces may prefer to isolate vignettes planted with warm hues, separated from other color harmonies by lots of foliage.

❦ In spring, before the garden's buffering green foliage has fully emerged, hot colors need careful treatment to avoid looking harsh. In fact, throughout the season, brilliant colors are enhanced by contrasting foliage. For example, dark green yews cool a stand of fiery salvia; pewter-grey artemisia tones down tangerine California poppies (*Eschscholzia californica*); the fresh lime-green of

hosta leaves illuminates a glade of scarlet begonias; and the buff spikes of feather reed grass (*Calamagrostis* spp.) complement the black-eyed Susans (*Rudbeckia hirta*) of late summer.

❦ Other ornamental grasses with brown-tone blades or inflorescences are outstanding in the hot garden — coppery leather leaf sedge (*Carex buchananii*), the fountain grasses (*Pennisetum* spp.) and northern sea oats (*Chasmanthium latifolium*), to name a few. And don't overlook the way purple-bronze foliage effectively tones down hot colors — purple smoke tree (*Cotinus coggygria* 'Royal Purple') is a good example.

❦ Hot colors look good set against green foliage or in front of fences or walls painted chocolate brown, taupe or dull green. But reddish-brown or redwood-stained fences need a buffer of green foliage between them and a border of hot-color flowers.

❦ If your garden is relentlessly bright and sunny, you'll find hot colors bear up better than blues or pinks; this is

A classic deep-red rose in full bloom ▲

Tulips ▲

not surprising when you consider that many hot-color plants originated in sunny spots like Mexico and South America. They blaze in the midday sun and glow like embers in the shadows of late day.

❧ If the setting is shady, you can still choose a range of hot-color plants, from globeflowers (*Trollius* spp.), daylilies and cardinal flowers (*Lobelia cardinalis*) to Asiatic lilies, bee balm (*Monarda* spp.) and tuberous begonias.

❧ As well as flowers and foliage, be sure to consider warm-tone berries and fruit, such as holly (*Ilex* spp.), crab apples (*Malus* spp.), mountain ash

(*Sorbus* spp.), winterberry (*Ilex verticillata*), pyracantha and cotoneaster; they also add structure to the garden. And don't forget fall's leaves, especially serviceberry (*Amelanchier* spp.), burning bush (*Euonymus alata*), maple (*Acer* spp.) and sumac (*Rhus* spp.).

SO WHAT'S HOT? *And* WHAT'S NOT?

The torrid orange butterfly weed (*Asclepias tuberosa*) is, but the 'Tropicana' hybrid tea rose is not — it's too pink. The tall 'Gold Plate' yarrow (*Achillea filipendulina*) is hot, but its paler cousin, 'Moonshine', is not. Also hot is the brick-color daylily (*Hemerocallis fulva*); the lovely lemon daylily (*H. citrina*) is not. Thread-leaved tickseed (*Coreopsis verticillata* 'Golden Shower') falls in the hot category, but the lemony 'Moonbeam' does not. Scarlet Oriental poppies (*Papaver orientale*) are definitely hot, so is spring's cascading basket-of-gold (*Aurinia saxatilis*) and late-summer's tall, burnished sneezeweed (*Helenium autumnale*). In other words, all the warm, bright colors that run the range from scarlet through orange and bronze into golden-yellow are hot.

The PINK GARDEN

If there's one request a garden designer hears more than any other, it's this: "I'd love a romantic garden in pinks and mauves, with maybe a little purple, too..."
That the pink garden has become a cliché in design is hardly surprising, given the enormous variety of outstanding plants from which to choose. And pink seems to embrace a range of tints and shades that is visually and emotionally pleasing to many of us.

❧ If pale pink is used extensively in a garden, the scene is enhanced by planting more intense pinks or purple-pinks

Delicate lavender-colored delphiniums and luscious peonies, in vibrant rose and the palest pink (above), make a romantic summer bouquet.

nearby. For example, the native bergamot (*Monarda fistulosa*) can look insipid alone, but wonderful backed by raspberry-pink hollyhocks, with crimson nicotiana at its base.

❧ Skillful use of foliage is needed in a pink garden — blue or grey is especially effective. Blue spruces or junipers provide "bones" while blue oat grass (*Helictotrichon sempervirens*), glaucous hostas such as *H. tokudama* or *H. sieboldiana* 'Elegans', lamb's-ears (*Stachys byzantina*), rue (*Ruta graveolens*) and the large family of artemisias are herbaceous possibilities. Dark or bright-green foliage works well, of course, but yellow-green is best used near mauve or purple-pink flowers. Deep wine tones like that of purple-leaf sand cherry (*Prunus* X *cistena*) or the red-leaved rose (*Rosa glauca* or *rubrifolia*) also enhance pink.

❧ A pink garden looks enchanting against a grey stone wall, a dark yew hedge or a white picket fence, but wages war in front of a red-orange brick wall or redwood fence.

❧ Pink includes that palest of tints known as blush, found in the excellent climbing rose 'New Dawn' or the mauve-throated blooms of *Magnolia* X *soulangiana*. Or it

can be the shimmery pink of the mallow 'Silver Cup' (*Lavatera*), with its hollyhock-like flowers. Like white flowers, pale pink ones illuminate the night garden.

❧ Hot pinks abound — the cold-hardy rhododendron 'Olga' lends a note of unabashed cheer to May gardens, and the 'Orbit' series of bedding geraniums (*Pelargonium*

spp.) features one called — what else? — 'Hot Pink'. The 'Super Elfin' impatiens called 'Lipstick' is another pink sizzler, described as a hot rose-pink.

❧ Good, clear pinks abound, from primroses to old roses to Rose-of-Sharon (*Hibiscus syriacus*). There's the feathery astilbe 'Rheinland', the lovely old peony 'Jules Elie' and the Michaelmas daisy 'Harrington's Pink' (*Aster nova-angliae*). Other pure pinks include the flowering Japanese cherry 'Kanzan' (*Prunus serrulata*), summer phlox 'Dodo Hanbury Forbes' (*Phlox paniculata*), flowering almond (*Prunus triloba*) and the tall grandiflora rose 'Queen Elizabeth'.

❧ It sometimes seems that seed companies and garden writers are intentionally confusing when they interchange terms like lilac, lavender and mauve. But where the first two correctly belong to the realm of the blues, the latter is most definitely a pink mixed with a little blue-violet. Mauve-pink flowers include the elegant clematis 'Comtesse de Bouchaud', the French lilac 'Belle de Nancy' and the lovely star-flowered allium, *A. christophii*.

❧ Magenta is really red with a big helping of purple, and one of those intense colors that gardeners either love or detest. It's seen in the hardy rhododendron 'P.J.M.' and the black-centered flowers of Armenian cranesbill (*Geranium psilostemon*). Although classed as pink, magenta needs careful placement in the garden; it's best used by itself with lots of buffering green or grey foliage, or to bring out magenta highlights in neighboring flowers.

❧ Other pink shades needing careful placement cover the range from peach to salmon and coral. While these flowers are theoretically too yellow for a refined pink theme, you may still choose to include a peach-pink tall bearded iris like 'Beverley Sills', a salmon-pink tulip like 'Elizabeth Arden', a coral-pink shrub like flowering quince (*Chaenomeles* spp.) or a fluorescent coral rose like 'Tropicana' in your pink garden.

❧ As clear pink deepens, it moves through the cerise-pink seen in the thornless Bourbon climbing rose 'Zéphirine Drouhin' and the versatile spirea 'Anthony Waterer' (*Spiraea* X *bumalda*). Then comes the crimson of Japanese maple 'Crimson Queen' (*Acer palmatum*) or velvety sweet William 'Dunnet's Dark Crimson' (*Dianthus barbatus*). At its deepest, pink appears maroon — like the unusual hollyhock 'Nigra' (*Alcea rosea*), the black tulip 'Queen of the Night' or the chocolate-scented perennial cosmos (*C. atrosanguineus*), described as darkest garnet.

Summer Phlox ▲
(P. paniculata)

China Pinks (Dianthus chinensis)

Hollyhock (Alcaea rosa)　　　　*Astilbe* (A. X arendsii)　　　　*Purple Coneflower* (Echinacea purpurea)

Blue Onion (Allium caerulea) ▲

Monkshood (Aconitum *spp.*) ▲

BLUE *in the* GARDEN

In the garden, blue flowers have an almost mystical appeal, owing more to sensuous color than to form. Think of an April sea of azure scilla, a rich purple haze of sage (*Salvia* X *superba*) or clouds of lavender catmint (*Nepeta* X *faassenii*). Certain blues planted in drifts have an ethereal effect, melting boundaries and suggesting shadows. On the other hand, blue can be intense and startling. Consider the translucent, pure hue of the temperamental Himalayan blue poppy (*Meconopsis betonicifolia*) or the equally blue but more readily grown common morning glory (*Ipomoea tricolor*).

Pure, clear blues are rare, and the shades embraced by the word "blue" do not always combine harmoniously: for example, it's better to separate violet-blue and clear blue, making generous use of complementary contrasts in soft yellow and peach. Since blue plantings tend to recede, this can be useful if you wish to make a garden longer or a bed more distant. For greater appreciation, however, blue flowers should be planted for close viewing.

❧ Spring seems to offer the lion's share of blue and purple. The little bulbs — *Scilla, Puschkinia, Chionodoxa* and *Muscari* — look lovely with daffodils and link the strident colors of early tulips. Other blues,

like forget-me-nots (*Myosotis sylvatica*), Virginia bluebells (*Mertensia virginica*), the elegant blue columbine (*Aquilegia caerulea*) and sparkling lavender-blue wild phlox (*P. divaricata*), are enhanced by the fresh green of emerging foliage.

❧ Late spring and early summer bring tall bearded iris in glistening lavender and purple, false indigo (*Baptisia australis*), lupines, perennial cornflower (*Centaurea montana*), Siberian iris, and peach-leaf bellflower (*Campanula persicifolia*). Wisteria, with its lavender racemes of bloom in June, can be considered a member of the blue family, as can the lavender *Clematis macropetala*.

❧ Blue annuals for season-long bloom are plentiful — lavender and purple pansies, lobelia, blue salvia (*S. farinacea* 'Victoria'), violet-purple browallia, love-in-a-mist (*Nigella damascena*), Chinese forget-me-not (*Cynoglossum amabile*), borage, violet-blue cupflower (*Nierembergia hippomanica* var. *violacea*), baby blue-eyes (*Nemophila menziesii*) and larkspur (*Consolida ambigua*).

❧ Perennial geraniums such as *Geranium* X 'Johnson's Blue' and the deep violet *G. ibericum* var. *platypetalum* make lovely companions to the white, pink and orange tones of peonies and Oriental poppies. Stately delphiniums add height.

◀ *Jacob's Ladder*
(Polemonium *spp.*)

Long-leaved Speedwell ▶
(Veronica longifolia)

Clockwise from top left: Delphiniums; Morning Glory (Ipomoea tricolor); *Rocky Mountain Columbine* (Aquilegia caerulea).

In summer, rush-like foliage discloses the pretty flowers of the hybrid spiderwort (*Tradescantia* X *andersoniana*) — and no blue summer garden would be complete without at least one spiked speedwell (*Veronica spicata*), such as 'Blue Peter' or 'True Blue'. Balloon flower (*Platycodon grandiflorus*) has lovely, pale blue flowers and balloon-like buds. Two unusual perennials are prickly sea holly (*Eryngium amethystinum*) and the tall globe thistle 'Taplow Blue' (*Echinops humilis*), with spiky silver-blue flowerheads. Clematis offers a number of suitable species and hybrids.

Summer ends with hauntingly lovely monkshoods (*Aconitum* spp.), and Michaelmas daisies such as *Aster novibelgii* 'Harrison's Blue' and purple 'Eventide' last well into fall. The easily grown *Caryopteris* X *clandonensis*, a shrub commonly known as bluebeard or blue spirea, has icy-blue flower spikes beloved by bees.

And don't forget blue-grey foliage. Excellent foils include blue spruce, juniper, Russian olive (*Elaeagnus angustifolia*), blue oat grass (*Helictotrichon sempervirens*), blue fescue (*Festuca ovina* var. *glauca*) and blue-tone hostas.

USING YELLOW

Next to white, yellow is the brightest hue in the gardener's palette. Red flowers may appear closer, but yellow ones are noticed first. Although yellow is not as emotionally complex as red (with its advancing intensity) or blue (with its moody haziness), a yellow garden can be optically confusing — a shimmery brilliance without nuance or definition — unless the eye can also rest on something less demanding. Adroit use of green or grey foliage, cream and buff flowers, and complementary contrasts of blue-violet, lavender and purple allow all the spectral variations of yellow to intermingle happily.

❧ Spring, of course, is when yellow predominates — with tiny fringed aconites (*Eranthis hyemalis*), species crocus, narcissus, tulips and yellow crown imperial (*Fritillaria imperialis*). Spring shrubs include forsythia and witch hazel (*Hamamelis*).

❧ But spring yellows can be glaring if not mitigated by contrasting blues. Forsythia and early dwarf tulips are enchanting with a carpet of scilla (*S. sibirica*) or glory-of-the-snow (*Chionodoxa lucilliae*). Narcissus and late-blooming tulips look lovely surrounded by grape hyacinths (*Muscari*).

❧ Blue works well with yellow in the summer garden, too, though the fuller foliage of the season balances the brighter hue. Fans of bearded iris might want to try a lemon-yellow variety with a tall, brilliant blue Italian bugloss (*Anchusa azurea*). Other blue-yellow marriages include a pale yellow yarrow (*Achillea* X 'Moonshine') with lavender *Geranium* X 'Johnson's Blue', and butter-yellow evening primrose (*Oenothera tetragona*) and vivid yellow Asiatic lilies with blue lupines or delphiniums.

Clockwise from top left: Goldenchain Tree (Laburnum watereri 'Vossii');

Evening Primrose (Oenothera tetragona), *Yellow Iris* (I. X germanica) *with blue Delphiniums; and Annual Marguerite* (Chrysanthemum frutescens).

❧ The easiest way to deploy the yellow arsenal is to select a few hardworking daisies. Easily grown in full sun, they tend to be drought-tolerant, too. For summer, there's tickseed (*Coreopsis grandiflora*) and its more refined cousin, thread-leaved coreopsis (*C. verticillata*). As well, we have golden marguerite (*Anthemis tinctoria*), annual marguerite (*Chrysanthemum frutescens*, now *Argyranthemum*), sunflowers (*Helianthus* spp.) and heliopsis (*H. helianthoides* subsp. *scabra*). Black-eyed Susan (*Rudbeckia hirta*) is highly recommended, especially the cultivar 'Goldsturm'. For late summer, choose yellow sneezeweed (*Helenium autumnale*) and the tall green-cone rudbeckia (*R. nitida*).

❧ Though yellow is primarily the color of sunny gardens, many good yellows do well in shade — globeflower (*Trollius* spp.), lemon daylily (*Hemerocallis flava*), the native lily (*Lilium canadense*), early primrose (*Primula vulgaris*) and luscious tuberous begonias.

❧ Chartreuse adds an interesting element — frothy lady's-mantle (*Alchemilla mollis*), annual nicotine (*Nicotiana alata* 'Nicki Lime') and *Hosta* 'August Moon' (among other yellow-green hostas).

❧ Don't overlook the luminous impact made by the yellow-gold foliage of shrubs. Consider golden privet (*Ligustrum* X *vicaryi*), golden plume elder (*Sambucus racemosa* 'Sutherland Gold'), yellow-edge dogwood (*Cornus alba* 'Spaethii') and 'Goldmound' spirea (*Spiraea japonica*). Gold-foliage shrubs tend to make a stronger "yellow" impact than green shrubs with yellow flowers, such as potentilla or Japanese kerria.

❧ Excellent yellow-gold evergreens include many spreading junipers, dwarf golden yew and golden globe cedar. Broad-leaf evergreens include many gold forms of wintercreeper euonymus (*E. fortunei*).

❧ Large-scale effects can be achieved with trees — the 'Sunburst' locust (*Gleditsia triacanthos* var. *inermis*) or the yellow-leaf form of black locust (*Robinia pseudoacacia* 'Frisia'), for instance.

❧ Yellow might also be fragrant, like the May-blooming clove or buffalo currant (*Ribes odoratum*), the wonderfully perfumed azalea 'Narcissiflora' or July's towering golden trumpet lilies. And yellow can be a plain-Jane, as in pansies, marigolds and zinnias, or an exotic beauty, revealed in the fragile blossoms of the Chinese tree peony (*Paeonia suffruticosa*).

The WHITE GARDEN

White flowers against green foliage have a stark, elegant beauty. No riot of color — just a sensuous, restful contrast, much like that found in the woods in spring. A garden that's filled with color by day recedes into the shadows after dark, but flowers that are white emerge from the darkness. Framed by their foliage, they shimmer with a magical, other-worldly quality and fill the air with intoxicating scents. Of all flowers, white ones deliver the most fragrance (orange to scarlet ones are the least scented). With the right choice of flowers, a white garden can soothe the eyes by day and excite the senses by night.

Oriental Lily 'Everest' (Lilium orientalis) ▲
◀ *A white garden, in all its summer glory.*
Flowering Tobacco (Nicotiana alata) ▼

For white flowers in spring, plant the snowy white perennial candytuft (*Iberis sempervirens*) alongside tall white tulips and a pale narcissus — 'Mount Hood', perhaps.

Scented lily-of-the-valley (*Convallaria majalis*) is pretty in a shaded corner of the garden. Blossoming fruit trees such as pear or white-flowered crab apple nicely frame the spring constellations and add a subtle perfume to the air. Don't overlook *Deutzia gracilis*, a carefree, though not perfumed, small shrub that grows 36 inches (90 cm) tall

with clusters of white florets. And no May garden would be complete without the fragrance of lilacs; white double-flowered 'Madame Lemoine' is a good choice.

June is peony time. Plant 'Festiva Maxima', which is both white and fragrant, with a Siberian iris like 'Fourfold White'. If you're into pyrotechnics, gas plant (*Dictamnus albus*) is reputed to exude a volatile oil that ignites when a lighted match is held nearby on a windless summer night. The leaves of the plant also have a faint scent of lemon.

Fruit trees for the white garden include the pear and white-flowered crab apple.

❧ Two families of June-flowering shrubs, both white and sweetly fragrant, are mock orange (*Philadelphus* spp.) and viburnum (*V. X carlcephalum*, *V. carlesii* and *V. X burkwoodii*). And be sure to include an old rose — any of the alba roses has unforgettable fragrance and would be the epitome of romance in your garden at night. A vine with showy blooms but less perfume is the double clematis 'Duchess of Edinburgh'.

❧ At the height of summer, perennials reach full bloom. Foremost among them are intoxicatingly fragrant regal lilies (*Lilium regale*); also showy but without perfume are white delphiniums such as the cultivar 'Galahad', shasta daisies (*Chrysanthemum X superbum*, now *Leucanthemum*), waving wands of black snakeroot (*Cimicifuga racemosa*) with its white flowers, and feathery spires of the astilbe 'Bridal Veil'.

❧ The annuals you set out in May should be coming into their own in June. White petunias, sweet alyssum, white annual geraniums (*Pelargonium* spp.) and tall white cosmos enjoy full sun and add to the pleasure of the garden at night. For shady areas, a favorite old-fashioned annual is white nicotine or flowering tobacco (*Nicotiana alata*). A true nocturnal, the 36-inch (90 cm) tall plants with tubular flowers look a little unhappy until dusk, then they snap to attention, filling the garden with unbelievable fragrance. (Incidentally, since *N. alata* is a non-hybrid, you might try collecting some seed each fall; it will grow true to form next year.)

❧ Impatiens, the trusty soldier for shady gardens, has a number of white hybrids. They look lovely with white-margined hostas. In fact, any plant with white variegated leaves comes alive at night.

❧ Out-of-the-ordinary plants include *Geranium pratense* 'Silver Queen', gooseneck loosestrife (*Lysimachia clethroides*), — and stunning sea kale (*Crambe cordifolia*). Once it feels at home in your garden (set it against a dark hedge or fence as a backdrop), it grows to 6 feet (2 m), has huge bluish-green leaves at its base and flowers like giant baby's-breath.

❧ Shadowy corners can be illuminated by white-flowered vines. The luxuriant *Clematis montana* blooms reliably in southern British Columbia, with starry white flowers that climb 25 feet (8 m) up the nearest obliging tree or wall; 'Henryi' is hardy in colder areas. A vine that loves heat and sun but blooms only at night is the tropically fragrant annual moonflower vine (*Ipoema alba*).

❧ As summer wanes, the garden is still lush with the rose-tinted ivory trusses of the versatile shrub *Hydrangea paniculata* 'Grandiflora', better known as peegee hydrangea. Sweet autumn clematis (*C. paniculata*) and silver-lace vine (*Polygonum aubertii*) are frothy white-colored candidates for the fence or arbor.

❧ For late-summer and fall interest, the tall white phloxes 'Mt. Fujiyama' or 'White Admiral' add an ethereal quality to the garden at night. Also good: white obedient plant (*Physostegia virginiana* 'Alba') and tall, aster-like *Boltonia asteroides*. August-blooming white Oriental lilies are elegant and fragrant, especially 'Everest' or 'Imperial Silver'.

Smooth Hydrangea (Hydrangea arborescens)

White Lilac (Syringa vulgaris)

❧ Depending on when you planted its corm, the beautiful Ethiopian native, peacock orchid (*Acidanthera bicolor* 'Murieliae', now *Gladiolus callianthus*) with fragrant star-shape white flowers tipped with maroon, will still be blooming.

❧ And when the white of the first frost stills the sound of the crickets, the annual alyssum, white ornamental kale and pale snapdragons go gently into the crisp autumn night. Until next year.

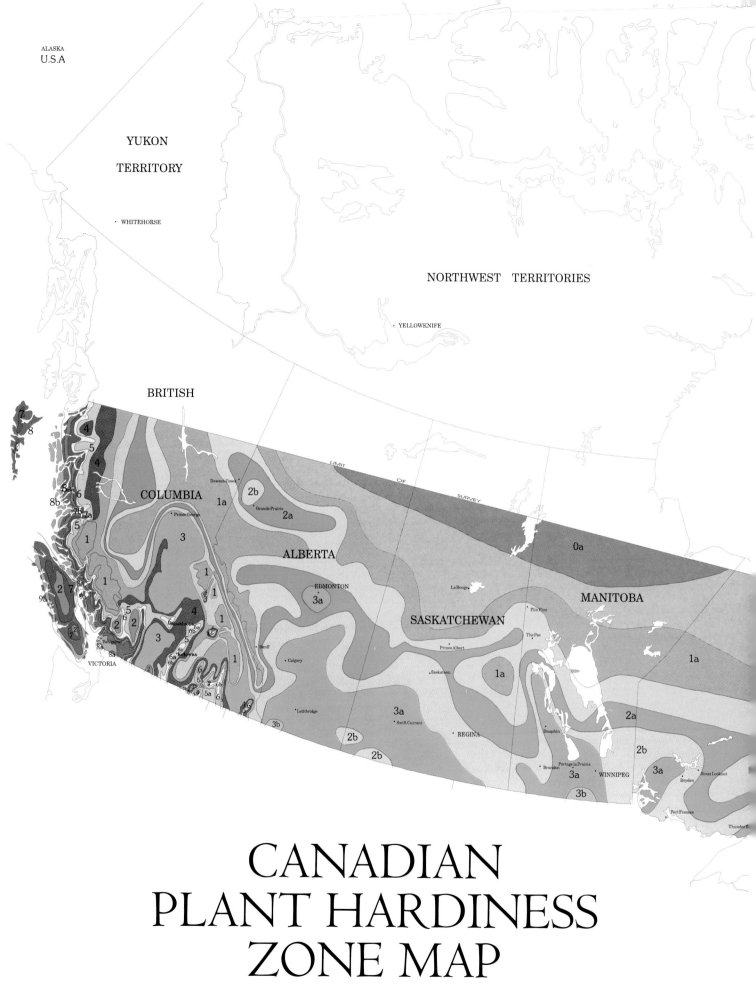

CANADIAN
PLANT HARDINESS
ZONE MAP

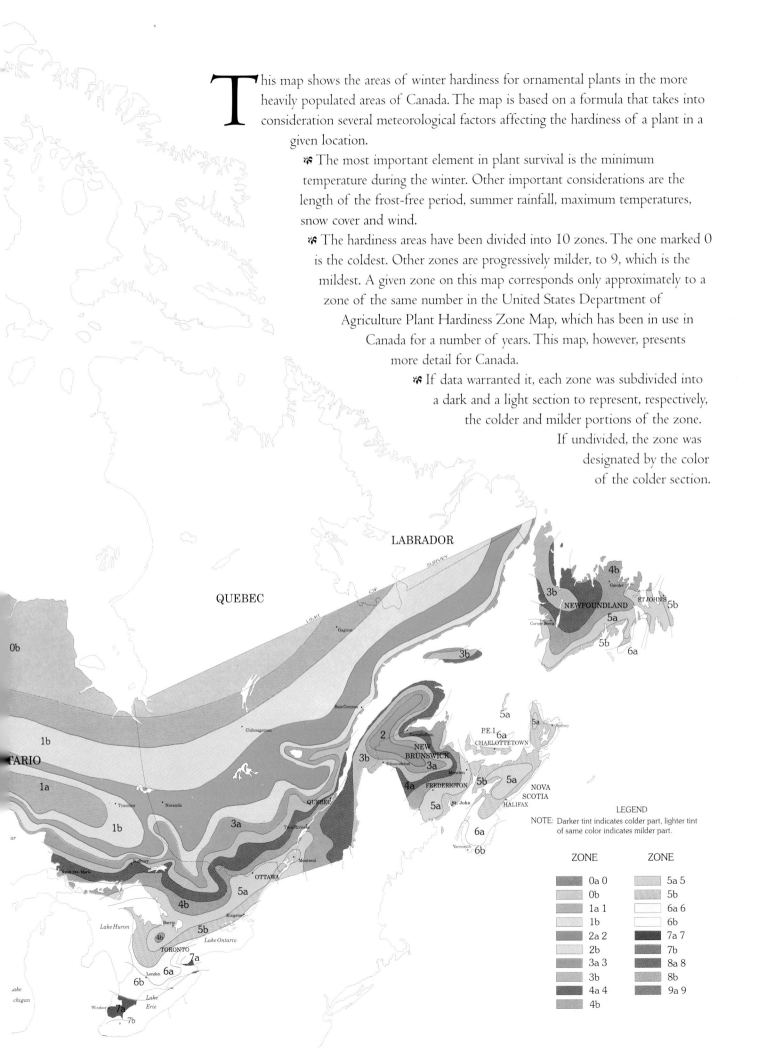

This map shows the areas of winter hardiness for ornamental plants in the more heavily populated areas of Canada. The map is based on a formula that takes into consideration several meteorological factors affecting the hardiness of a plant in a given location.

❧ The most important element in plant survival is the minimum temperature during the winter. Other important considerations are the length of the frost-free period, summer rainfall, maximum temperatures, snow cover and wind.

❧ The hardiness areas have been divided into 10 zones. The one marked 0 is the coldest. Other zones are progressively milder, to 9, which is the mildest. A given zone on this map corresponds only approximately to a zone of the same number in the United States Department of Agriculture Plant Hardiness Zone Map, which has been in use in Canada for a number of years. This map, however, presents more detail for Canada.

❧ If data warranted it, each zone was subdivided into a dark and a light section to represent, respectively, the colder and milder portions of the zone. If undivided, the zone was designated by the color of the colder section.

LABRADOR

QUEBEC

NEWFOUNDLAND

ONTARIO

NEW BRUNSWICK

NOVA SCOTIA

P.E.I.

LEGEND
NOTE: Darker tint indicates colder part, lighter tint of same color indicates milder part.

ZONE	ZONE
0a 0	5a 5
0b	5b
1a 1	6a 6
1b	6b
2a 2	7a 7
2b	7b
3a 3	8a 8
3b	8b
4a 4	9a 9
4b	

THE CONTRIBUTORS

LIZ PRIMEAU is the editor of *Canadian Gardening*. In her five years with the magazine, she has visited gardens in all parts of Canada and has heard firsthand from committed Canadian gardeners about what works — or doesn't work! — in this widely varied climate of ours. An avid and experienced gardener herself, she has also been a featured speaker at gardening conferences, trade shows and garden clubs. Liz Primeau writes regularly on gardening for *The Globe and Mail's* Design section, and has also worked as a writer and editor with *Weekend Magazine, Toronto Life, Chatelaine, City Woman, Vista* and *Ontario Living* during a 23-year journalistic career.

PENNY ARTHURS is a widely respected garden designer and the owner of her own design company, The Chelsea Gardener. She has designed city and country gardens in and around Toronto and across the country — many of which are featured on annual garden tours. A graduate of The English Gardening School, one of England's leading schools of garden design, Penny Arthurs writes regularly on garden design for *Canadian Gardening* and other magazines, and has also lectured and made television appearances on the subject.

TREVOR AND BRENDA COLE met as horticultural students at the Royal Botanical Gardens, Kew, in England. After graduating, they worked in several parks departments and nurseries before emigrating to Canada in 1967. Trevor then worked for Agriculture Canada as Curator of the Dominion Arboretum, retiring in 1995. He has also written two books — *The Ontario Gardener* (1991) and *Gardening with Trees and Shrubs* (spring 1996). Brenda is a freelance garden writer with a regular column in *The Ottawa Citizen* and the *North Bay Nugget.* Together they write a column of regional news for *Canadian Gardening* magazine.

Photographers

BRUCE THOMAS BARR: page 54.

MICHAEL BRAUER: pages 27 (top), 36, 63 (inset).

DAN CALLIS: page 10.

JANET DAVIS: pages 70 (right), 71 (left), 74, 75, 76, 77, 78, 79, 82, 84, 85, 87.

CHRISTOPHER DEW: back cover (right); pages 6, 17, 35, 38 (top), 41, 43 (top), 44, 46, 47, 52, 68, 80.

JIM EAGER: page 42.

FRANK KERSHAW: pages 24, 26 (top), 27 (middle), 48, 49, 50, 51, 53, 55, 56 (left), 59, 61 (left).

BERT KLASSEN: back cover (left); pages 1, 2-3, 4, 5 (photo of Liz Primeau), 16, 21, 25, 27 (bottom), 29, 31 (bottom right), 37, 56 (right), 57, 60, 61 (right), 63 (background).

JOHN MORRISON: page 7.

CLAUDE NOEL: page 40 (left).

JERRY SHULMAN: front cover; pages 14, 31 (top), 64, 66, 67, 69, 70 (left), 71 (right), 72, 83, 86.

LYNN THOMPSON: pages 43 (bottom), 65.

DAVID VENTRUDO: pages 28, 31 (bottom left), 32.

PADDY WALES: pages 8, 9, 11, 13, 18, 19, 20, 22, 23, 26 (bottom), 33, 38 (bottom), 39, 40 (right), 45, 73.

Illustrations on page 58 are by CAROL PATON.

The map of Canada's Plant Hardiness Zones (pages 87-88) was produced by the Centre for Land and Biological Resources Research, Research Branch, Agriculture Canada from information supplied by the Ottawa Research Station and the Meteorological Branch, Environment Canada 1993.

We would like to thank Bryan Monette and Ron St. John of the Research Branch for their kind help in supplying us with this material.

Acknowledgments

We are grateful to the many talented garden writers from across the country whose articles in *Canadian Gardening* magazine over the last six years have been an inspiration for this book series. These include Penny Arthurs, Trevor and Brenda Cole, Jo Currie, Janet Davis, Rebecca Hanes-Fox, Karen Hanley, Ross Hawthorne, Jean Innes, Elizabeth Irving, Jacqueline Jantunen, Barbara MacKay, Janet McNaughton, Gary Miller, Gillian Pritchard, Wayne Renaud, Anne Rhodes, Andrew Vowles and Paddy Wales.
❧ We are also indebted to the many Canadian gardeners from coast to coast who so generously shared their gardening successes with *Canadian Gardening* and provided the magazine with the wealth of stunning and inspirational photographs which appear throughout this book. Our thanks to Geoff Armstrong, Joan and Joel Brink, David Dombosky and Linda Dunlop, Sharon Edey, Doris Fancourt-Smith, Ilona and Michael Griffin,

Sandy and Elana Heard, Linda Janzen, Patrick Kelly, Sandy and Des Kennedy, Frank Kershaw, Patrick Lima and John Scanlon, Audrey Litherland, Barry More, Rosemary Pauer, Valerie and Carl Pfeiffer, Joe Souccar and Maureen Maguire, Julie Van Nostrand and Luc Wintzen. We would also like to thank Janis and David Weenen.
❧ In some cases, it was not possible to identify gardens or their owners from the photographs of garden details which appear throughout this book. We acknowledge them here and are grateful for the use of this material.

SPECIAL THANKS
❧ A book like this requires solid teamwork to make it a success, and it's my pleasure here to thank the members of our team. I'm especially indebted to Madison Press project editor Wanda Nowakowska, who gave unstintingly of her time and energy. Her vision and high standards are intrinsic to the book.

My warm thanks also goes to my co-worker, Rebecca Hanes-Fox, *Canadian Gardening's* managing editor. She's an invaluable ideas person and an integral part of the book — from its planning stages to the final manuscript. The contribution of our consultants, Penny Arthurs and Brenda and Trevor Cole, is also especially appreciated; they provided their advice and expertise whenever we needed it, and with good humor and enthusiasm throughout. Thanks, too, to Madison Press editor Ian Coutts, who pulled material together and paved the way for the work of others. Credit for the book's elegant look goes to Gord Sibley, who has an unerring eye for type and design, as well as to the photographers who provided us with the inspiring images featured in the book. Lastly, my thanks to the magazine's editorial director, Tom Hopkins, and its publisher, Phil Whalen. Their support and commitment to the project are very much appreciated. — *Liz Primeau*

Selected Bibliography

❧ Allison, James. *Water in the Garden.* Boston/Toronto: Little, Brown and Company Limited, 1991.

❧ Brookes, John. *John Brookes' Garden Design Book.* Montreal: RD Press, 1991.

❧ Hobhouse, Penelope. *Color in Your Garden.* Boston/Toronto: Little, Brown and Company Limited, 1989.

❧ Keen, Mary. *Gardening with Color.* Toronto: Octopus Publishing Group, 1991.

❧ Nash, Helen. *The Pond Doctor.* New York: Sterling Publishing Co. Inc., 1994.

❧ Seike, Kiyoshi, Masanobu Kudo and David Engel. *A Japanese Touch for Your Garden.* Tokyo: Kodansha International Ltd, 1980.

❧ Tarrant, David, and the Editors of *Canadian Gardening. David Tarrant's Canadian Gardens.* Vancouver/Toronto: Whitecap Books, 1994.

INDEX

Design
    garden elements, 15
    garden styles, 12
    principles, 9-15
    scale plan, 9
    site evaluation, 10
Dianthus chinensis, 74
Dogwood
    red-osier, *49*
    siberian, 51
    tatarian, 49
Dracaena, 27
Dusty miller, 27
Dwarf cattail, 62

E

Echeveria, 37
Echinacea purpurea, 50, 75
Echinops humilis, 79
Edging
    formal, 26, *26,* 27
    ponds, 60-61
Eichornia crassipes, 61
Elaeagnus angustifolia, 79
Elodea, 62
Eranthis hyemalis, 51
Eryngium amethystinum, 79
Eschscholzia californica, 70
Espaliered tree, 42
Euonymus, 27
    E. alata, 32, 49, 71
    E. fortunei, 32, 42, 48
    'Goldspot', 51
    'Emerald Gaiety', 51
Evening primrose, 81
Evergreens, 47, 48, 49
    yellow-gold, 83

F

Fairy moss, 61
Feather reed grass, 70
Fences, *18, 20,* 38, 42,
    44, 47
    bamboo, 32
    decoration, 42
    formal, 24, 26
    in a Japanese garden, 32
    pickets, *18, 20,* 21
    windows in, 44

Ferns, 30, 32
    Athyrium nipponicum
        'Pictum', 32
    Japanese painted, 32
Festuca glauca, 32
Firethorn, 32, 48
Fish, 54, 55, 62
    overwintering, 62
Flowering almond, 32
Flowering quince, 74
Flowering rush, 62
Focal point, 40
    water, 54
    formal, 26
Foliage plants, 41, 43
Forget-me-not, 23
Formal gardens, 24-27
Fountain grass, 70
Fountains, 15, 26, 45
Fritillaria imperialis, 81
Furniture, 15, 44
    cottage garden, 21
    formal garden, 26
    Japanese garden, 31
    Mediterranean, 37
    small urban garden, 45

G

Garden design
    cottage, 21
    focal point, 40
    formal, 24
    Japanese, 28-33
    Mediterranean, 34
    small urban, 38-45
Garden furniture, 15, 21,
    26, 31, 37, 44, 45
Garden ornaments, 26, *26,*
    30, 32, 36, 40, 45
Garden plan, 47
Garden sheds, 36, 48
Garden structures, 34, 45
Garden styles, 12
Gardens
    cottage, 18-23
    elements, 15
    formal, 24-27
    Japanese, 28-33
    in winter, 46-51

maintenance, 22, 30, 40
    Mediterranean, 34-37
    small, 38-45
    styles, 12
Gates
    cottage, *8,* 21
    formal, 26
    wrought-iron, 45, 47
Gaultheria procumbens, 32
Gazebos, 15, 26, 45
Geranium, 32, 40
    G. 'Johnson's Blue', 81
    G. pratense 'Silver
        Queen', 87
    G. psilostemon, 74
Gleditsia, 32
Globe thistle, 79
Globeflower, 71, 82
Glory-of-the-snow, 81
Golden marguerite, 82
Gooseneck loosestrife, 87
Grape hyacinth, 23, 81
Grasses
    blue oat, 72
    feather reed, 70
    fountain, 70
    northern sea oats, 70
    ornamental, 32, 41, *49,*
        50, 70
Ground cover, 22, 30,
    32, 41

H

Hamamelis, 81
Hedera helix, 32
    'Baltica', 51
Hedges, 15 , 24, *24,*
    47, 48
    formal, 27
    Japanese garden, 32
    white cedar, 48
Helenium autumnale, 71, 82
Helianthus, 82
Helichrysum petiolare, 40
Helictotrichon sempervirens,
    72, 79
Heliopsis, 82
Heliotrope, 40
Hemerocallis
    H. citrina, 71, 23
    H. flava, 82
    H. fulva, 71

Hemlock, 48
Herb garden, 21
Herbs, 23, 34, 36, 37
Hibiscus syriacus, 73
Highbush cranberry,
    48, 49
Holly, 48, 51, 71
Hollyhock, *7,* 22, 23,
    72, 75
    'Nigra', 74
Honey locust, 32
Honeysuckle, 43
Hosta, 24, 27, 32, 41, 45,
    70, 79
    H. 'August Moon', 82
    H. sieboldiana 'Elegans', 72
    H. tokudama, 72
    in a Japanese garden, *29*
Hyacinth, 37
Hydrangea, 50, *50*
    climbing, 43
    H. anomala petiolaris, 43
    H. arborescens, 87
    H. paniculata
        'Grandiflora', 87
    H. paniculata, 32
    H. quercifolia, 32

I

Iberis sempervirens, 85
Ilex, 71
    I. verticillata, 71
    I. X meserveae 'Blue
        Prince', 51
    I. X meserveae 'Blue
        Princess', 51
Ipoema alba, 87
Ipomoea, 43
    I. tricolor, 78
Iris
    'Beverley Sills', 74
    I. ensata, 62
    I. X germanica, 83
    Japanese, 32, 62
    siberian, 32
Italian bugloss, 81
Ivy, 22, 26, 27, 32
    English, 42

EDITORIAL DIRECTOR   Hugh Brewster

PROJECT EDITOR   Wanda Nowakowska

EDITORIAL ASSISTANCE   Rebecca Hanes-Fox

PRODUCTION DIRECTOR   Susan Barrable

PRODUCTION COORDINATOR   Sandra L. Hall

BOOK DESIGN AND LAYOUT   Gordon Sibley Design Inc.

PRINTING AND BINDING   Tien Wah Press

CANADIAN GARDENING'S
CREATING A GARDEN
was produced by
Madison Press Books